Frank Rodgers

BATTLE FOR EYETOOTH

PUFFIN

PUFFIN BOOKS

Published by the Penguin Group
Penguin Books Ltd, 80 Strand, London WC2R 0RL, England
Penguin Group (USA) Inc., 375 Hudson Street, New York, New York 10014, USA
Penguin Group (Canada), 10 Alcorn Avenue, Toronto, Ontario, Canada M4V 3B2
(a division of Pearson Penguin Canada Inc.)
Penguin Ireland, 25 St Stephen's Green, Dublin 2, Ireland (a division of Penguin Books Ltd)
Penguin Group (Australia), 250 Camberwell Road,
Camberwell, Victoria 3124, Australia (a division of Pearson Australia Group Pty Ltd)
Penguin Books India Pvt Ltd, 11 Community Centre,
Panchsheel Park, New Delhi – 110 017, India
Penguin Group (NZ), cnr Airborne and Rosedale Roads, Albany,
Auckland 1310, New Zealand (a division of Pearson New Zealand Ltd)
Penguin Books (South Africa) (Pty) Ltd, 24 Sturdee Avenue,
Rosebank 2196, South Africa

Penguin Books Ltd, Registered Offices: 80 Strand, London WC2R 0RL, England

www.penguin.com

First published 2005
1

Text copyright © Frank Rodgers, 2005
Illustrations copyright © Chris Inns, 2005
All rights reserved

Set in 14/16.5 pt Adobe Sabon
Typeset by Rowland Phototypesetting Ltd, Bury St Edmunds, Suffolk
Made and printed in England by Clays Ltd, St Ives plc

British Library Cataloguing in Publication Data
A CIP catalogue record for this book is available from the British Library

ISBN 0–141–31616–0

For Zoë and Adam

Prologue

From the highest room of his castle's west tower Count Fibula watches the darkness slowly gather around the jutting rocks and rooftops of Eyetooth. Lifting a silver cup of rats' blood from an ancient oak table he takes a reflective sip. The failing light has a strangeness about it tonight – a murky, brooding quality that exactly matches his mood. A cobwebby mist, floating downwards, covers the spires, turrets and battlements with layers of wispy shrouds. A smile twitches at the corners of Fibula's thin dark lips. Yes, he muses, most appropriate. Spiderwebs are covering Eyetooth . . . and I am the spider.

Chapter One

The estate car grumbled its way up the pine-covered hill, hauling the rumbling bulk of the family's old caravan . . . with its strange and secret passengers.

Joe glanced over his shoulder. His two vampire friends, Count Muesli and Count Corpus, would be asleep in the caravan – stretched out on the narrow bunks on which they had sprinkled a little earth from their native mountain of Eyetooth.

I wonder if vampires dream? he thought. If they do they'll probably be dreaming of their return to Eyetooth . . . and the coming struggle to free their hidden vampire refuge from Fibula's evil grip.

In some ways Joe still could not believe all that had happened to him. Barely five weeks ago he and his family had been tricked into going up to Eyetooth by the malevolent Count Fibula. Although his family had been imprisoned, he himself had escaped. Helped by a young vegetarian vampire, Count Muesli, and his friend Count Corpus, he had managed to rescue his family from Fibula's bloodsucking clutches. Muesli and Corpus had to flee from Eyetooth too – and so, for five weeks, unknown to anyone outside the family, they had lived in Joe's attic.

Joe sighed. In a matter of hours he would once more be in the lonely wilds under the shadow of Eyetooth's mysterious mountain. His two vampire friends would leave on their dangerous mission and he would never see them again. Their adventure was continuing . . . but he felt his was over.

Joe sighed again, louder than he meant to, because his father glanced at him and said, 'Got to say goodbye sometime, Joe. Don't feel too good about it myself. Got sort of used to having a couple of vampires around the house.' He grinned as he changed gear. 'So did your mum.'

'I know,' Joe replied. 'Mum was sorry to

see them go . . . and Granny Roz would've come with us if she hadn't hurt her leg.'

Vinny laughed.

'What a battler my old mum is! What was it she said before we left?'

'"I want to go up to that Mr Fibula and blacken his eye."' Joe's imitation of his gran's voice was perfect and his dad chortled.

'I tried explaining that we were just going to drop Muesli and Corpus off at the mountain – that they would make their own way up to Eyetooth and we would go on to the film festival – but I don't think she believed me.' Vinny rolled his eyes. 'She says she's going to keep phoning my mobile just to make sure we're not going anywhere near Eyetooth.'

'That's Granny all right,' said Joe with a grin. He gazed out at the flickering branches of the pine forest, his smile slowly fading. 'I really wish we could help Muesli and Corpus fight against Fibula, Dad. I know it's impossible . . . but I just wish we could.'

'They have to do it on their own, Joe.'

'Yeah.' Joe stared glumly out of the window.

Vinny saw that his son's spirits needed a lift. 'Never mind,' he went on cheerily.

'*Vampires on Holiday* might do nicely at the festival. I can just see the headline: *New director cuts his teeth on great vampire comedy*.' He chortled. 'That would be great, wouldn't it?'

Joe smiled again despite himself. His dad had always been overly optimistic about the success of his short films, even though all his previous attempts had been flops. This time, however, thought Joe, he might really be on to something. *Vampires on Holiday* had turned out well. The footage that Vinny had shot of Fibula's black, horse-drawn hearse and his castle in Eyetooth had added real atmosphere. The whole film looked good and was actually very funny.

'Yeah, Dad. It would. It would be brilliant.'

He twisted round in his seat and looked through the back window at the old caravan, bumping and swaying behind them. 'I hope Muesli and Corpus are all right in there. The bunk beds are not exactly comfortable, are they?'

'A bit more comfortable than the coffins they sleep in up in Eyetooth, I would have thought,' said Vinny.

'Don't know about that, Dad,' replied Joe.

'Corpus was telling me about his. It's lined with padded silk. He says Muesli's coffin's the same. Sounds comfy enough to me.'

Vinny laughed, changing gear as he approached another bend. There was a sudden dull *clunk* from somewhere under the car and his laugh changed to a groan of exasperation. 'I don't believe it,' he muttered as he wiggled the now slack gear lever. 'Feels like the clutch cable has gone. We'll have to stop. Just when things were going so well. This means we won't get to Eyetooth tonight.'

Joe frowned anxiously as the car rolled on to the grass verge.

'So what can we do, Dad?'

Vinny rubbed his chin ruefully.

'It's not far to the town. I'll call the film-festival office. They'll be able to give me the number of a garage that can tow us in. Hopefully we'll be able to get the clutch repaired tomorrow.'

'But what about Muesli and Corpus?' asked Joe. 'They'll be stuck in the caravan.'

Vinny looked worried.

'I know,' he replied. 'And having Corpus in the caravan is like keeping a buzzard in a budgie cage.'

Chapter Two

It was early evening when the tow truck pulled the car and caravan up to a garage in the town.

'Good news, Joe,' Vinny said on his return to the car. 'It'll be fixed by tomorrow afternoon. I booked us a room in a hotel just across the square and the mechanic says he'll tow the caravan over to the hotel car park.'

'Do you think Mue–' Joe lowered his voice to a whisper, 'I mean *you know who* will be awake? Perhaps I should go in and tell them what's happening.'

Vinny stole a glance at the mechanic, who had finished disconnecting the caravan and was getting into his truck in order to tow the car into the garage.

'Good idea,' he replied. 'But make it quick.'

Joe nodded and slipped quickly out of the car.

Even with the blinds drawn, the interior of the caravan wasn't entirely dark, and Joe could see everything well enough.

Muesli and Corpus were lying on the narrow bunks on either side of the caravan. They were both wide awake. Wrapped in their black silk cloaks they stood out starkly against the bright, candy-coloured furnishings. Joe thought they looked as out of place as crows in a cake shop.

'Something has happened, hasn't it, Joe,' said Muesli quietly, his shock of orange hair making a strange silhouette against the drawn blind as he and Corpus sat up silently.

Joe quickly explained about the breakdown. 'The caravan's going to be towed to the hotel car park,' he said. 'I'm sorry but you'll have to spend the night in here.'

Corpus groaned in disappointment and pulled his black cloak tightly round him.

'It's frustrating, Corpy, but it seems it

can't be helped,' Muesli said, sighing. He turned back to Joe and smiled encouragingly. 'We'll be fine, don't worry.'

Corpus scratched his big, shaggy head. 'Don't much care for the idea of being cooped up for another day, Mooz,' he mumbled. 'I'm too big for such a small space. I'll knock something over. I need to get out and stretch my legs.' Swinging his legs over the edge of the bunk he planted his big feet on the floor and stood up.

Joe saw that Corpus had to stoop to prevent his head hitting the ceiling.

'I'm too big for this caravan,' Corpus repeated, sighing mournfully. 'If I stand up too quickly I'll raise a goosebump on the roof.'

'Take it easy, Corpy,' said Muesli, smiling. 'We'll just have to make the best of it. Sit tight tonight and tomorrow night we'll be in Eyetooth.' His expression became grim. 'It's been thirty-three days since we left, and all that time I willed my broken arm to mend and worried about what Fibula was doing. But you know how slowly things move in Eyetooth, Corpy. Fibula will not yet hold complete control, I'm sure of it. One more day shouldn't make a difference. By tomorrow night we'll be back where we belong and our battle to free our home from Fibula's clutches can begin.' He smiled again. 'Just one more day.'

Corpus slumped forward gloomily.

'I suppose so.' He sighed.

'Sorry but I'll have to go,' whispered Joe. 'I'll come back once we're settled in the hotel, OK?'

Muesli nodded.

'See you later then, Joe,' he said quietly.

Joe opened the door a crack, made sure the mechanic wasn't outside, slipped through and closed it behind him. Corpus shook his big head again dolefully.

'Don't like this, Mooz,' he muttered. 'Don't like it one little bit.'

Chapter Three

Joe and his dad carried their bags up a narrow wooden staircase to their small room at the top of the old hotel.

Vinny dumped the case on to his bed and Joe went over to the window.

'There's the caravan, Dad,' he cried, pointing down into the paved yard. 'They've left it by that tree.'

The caravan sat by the high side wall of the yard under the spreading branches of a huge chestnut tree. There were five cars and a red and black motorbike parked on the other side of the yard.

Vinny looked out too and nodded in approval.

'That'll do,' he said. 'Nicely shaded. Won't get hot if the sun shines tomorrow.'

'I hope Muesli manages to make Corpus stay indoors tonight,' mused Joe. 'Imagine anyone bumping into a huge vampire like him on a dark night – they'd take one look at his big eyes, fangs and wild hair and run a mile!'

Vinny's mobile phone rang.

'It's your gran,' he said as he picked it up. 'Hello, Roz. How are you feeling? How's the leg?'

Joe came over and Vinny held the phone between them. His granny had a habit of talking very loudly on the phone so he was able to hear every word.

'It's an annoyance, that's what it is,' replied Roz. 'If I didn't have this bad leg I could've come with you. Have you dropped Muesli and Corpus off yet?'

'Er . . . not yet,' replied Vinny. 'A slight hitch. Nothing serious. Just car trouble. We'll take them to the mountain tomorrow.'

A knock at the door made them both turn round.

'Someone at the door, Roz,' he said quickly. 'I'll call you back later and you can speak to Joe, OK?'

13

Vinny answered the door to find a tall girl holding a pile of folded towels. She was about seventeen with short, dark hair and widely set, intense blue eyes under thick, finely arched dark brows.

'I'm Anthonia,' she said, handing over the towels. 'I look after this floor. Your bathroom is just opposite.'

'Thank you, Anthonia,' replied Vinny, beginning to close the door.

'On holiday, are you?' the girl asked. 'Well, sort of,' replied Vinny. He opened the door again, not wanting to appear rude.

Joe joined his dad by the door. 'We're here for the film festival,' he said proudly. 'My dad's film comedy, *Vampires on Holiday*, is being shown.'

Joe noticed a curious look flick across Anthonia's face. 'We're only staying here one night,' Vinny told her. 'Until the car's fixed. Then we're going to stay in a camp-site just outside town.'

'Will you be going into the mountains?' the girl asked.

'Why do you want to know?' Joe said quickly, suddenly uneasy.

'It's just that the mountains are not

14

exactly good for camping in,' Anthonia went on. 'A bit wild. Dangerous, some say. Haven't you heard that?'

'Oh yes, but it doesn't bother us,' retorted Vinny breezily. 'We've been there on holiday before, haven't we, Joe?' He felt his son nudge him sharply in the back. 'Well, that is . . . we didn't go very far into the mountains – just pottered around the edge.'

'Ah,' said the girl and looked at Joe. Joe felt his neck start to colour under her gaze. He got the feeling that she knew Vinny had told a fib.

'I find the mountains fascinating,' was all she said.

'Well, that's nice,' Vinny offered lamely in return. He smiled at the girl and started to close the door again. 'So, anyway, thanks for the towels, Anthonia.'

This time the girl stepped back.

'If we need anything we'll call for you, then?' said Vinny.

Anthonia nodded and turned away. 'Yes. Do that.'

Vinny closed the door and Joe made a face.

'She was a bit weird, wasn't she, Dad?'

'A bit,' mused Vinny mildly, shaking his head. 'Strange girl. Very Strange.'

Chapter Four

When Joe ran downstairs about half an hour later there was no sign of Anthonia. He was glad, as he didn't relish the thought of another conversation with her. There was something about the look in her eyes that bothered him. She's too intense for me, he thought.

It was getting dark as Joe came out of the back door of the hotel into the yard. An old lamp above the door cast a pool of yellow light over the steps and Joe was pleased to see that it made the rest of the yard look even darker. The vague, dark-brown, whale-like hump of the caravan was almost lost in the deep shadows of the wall and the big tree. Making sure there was no one around, Joe ran quickly across the yard, ducked round the side of the caravan and, knocking quietly, unlocked the door and slipped through. Muesli and Corpus were sitting opposite each other across the narrow table, playing cards in the dim light. 'Everything all right?' whispered Muesli.

'Yes.' Joe began to make out the vampires' pale features as his eyes adjusted to the gloom. 'Dad thinks it might be OK for you to stretch your legs outside later tonight if you're careful.' Joe saw Corpus's face split in a grin and added quickly, 'But just outside the door, between the caravan and the wall. That way you can't be seen from the hotel.'

'Just the ticket!' said Corpus gleefully.

'We'll wait until well after midnight,' Muesli reassured him quietly. 'Just to make sure.'

'Be careful,' whispered Joe, unable to stop himself glancing anxiously at Corpus. He saw Muesli smile.

'Don't worry, we will.'

Chapter Five

Fibula watched night fall over Eyetooth from the narrow window of his lofty tower room. He gave a little shiver of pleasure as he imagined his power spreading out from the mountain to the world beyond – imagined his vampires bringing back human captives to Eyetooth. He was very pleased. His plans were working out well. Soon, he knew, there would be no one left in Eyetooth to oppose him.

A soft rustle of wings made him look up. Bats that had made their home in that cold, windy room flitted and darted into the dusk. Fibula smiled. They were like his dark thoughts, flying out from the castle to the world beyond.

Fibula watched them for a moment before making his way back down the spiral stone staircase.

In the great hall he found his servant, Ichor, tending the fire. The squat little figure was carefully prodding two lonely, smouldering logs in the enormous grate, trying to coax out a few more warming flames.

As Fibula paused in the shadows by the door he saw Ichor glance longingly at the basket of logs he had just brought in and stretch out a tentative hand.

'No more logs!' commanded Fibula sharply, making Ichor jump and withdraw his hand guiltily. 'I've told you before. Two is quite sufficient.'

'Yes, Master,' replied Ichor, rubbing his cold hands together. 'Two it is.' He turned his broad beam to the pitiful warmth of the fitful flames and watched as his master sank into his throne-like chair at the head of the great table. As Ichor waited for Count Fibula to speak he cast his eyes around the room in which he had served for so many years – the room in which he had never been warm. Large, dusty wrought-iron candle sconces stood on either side of the huge stone fireplace. Their dripping candles cast a guttering glow that barely reached the table in the centre of the cold, flagstoned floor. Above the table hung three enormous candelabra that were looped with grimy cobwebs like grey seaweed on an ancient wreck.

Fibula's face was shadowed but Ichor could see the occasional flame reflected in his master's hooded eyes. The servant shifted his weight from one foot to the other.

The watching eyes glittered.

'Er . . . Scabrus and Crusst are organizing the curfew patrols for tonight, Master,' he ventured at last. 'They've been quite successful so far. One rebel caught after eight o'clock last night and two the night before.'

Count Fibula already knew this but he smirked nevertheless. He was always pleased when things went his way.

'Yes,' he hissed softly. 'It's a good excuse for locking up dissenters, isn't it? Anyone found outdoors after eight will be jailed. It won't be long before all of the opposition are behind bars. The plotters are being reduced steadily, day by day.'

'There are a few important ones still on the loose, Master,' remarked Ichor.

Fibula shot him an angry glance.

'Stating the obvious again, aren't you, Ichor?' he snarled. 'It's a bad habit.'

'Sorry, Master,' mumbled Ichor, shuffling his feet nervously. 'I just meant –'

'I know what you meant, fool!' snapped Fibula. 'Muesli's closest friends are still at large.' He snatched up a parchment from the table and cast his narrowed eyes over the list written on it. 'Darceth, Krazul, Bray, Alchema – all still have their freedom!' He flung the parchment aside, lip curling. 'Where are they? Surely they can't be too hard to find?' He glowered. 'I have a special score to settle with Alchema. An unfinished fight.'

Ichor flinched under Fibula's glare but his master turned his baleful gaze to the fire.

'Horba and Spitz tell me a meeting of my enemies is planned for tomorrow night in the tunnels,' Fibula murmured, half to himself.

'That's good, isn't it, Master?' Ichor ventured hopefully.

Fibula's face contorted as he turned to stare at his servant again.

'Is it? *Is it?*' he screeched. 'It's a warren down there! A honeycomb! A Swiss cheese!

We've had intelligence before that meetings were planned in the tunnels and did we find them? No, we did not! Our patrols wandered around for hours. They got lost eventually. There are hundreds of tunnels and most of them are dead ends. Took the patrols two days to find their way back to the surface.'

'Y-yes,' stammered Ichor. 'I know, Master. But surely Spitz knows the correct location this time?'

Count Fibula pulled his black cloak round him and leant back, fixing his servant with a bleak stare.

'He'd better,' he hissed. 'I made him one of my chiefs of police but I could just as easily have him thrown in a dungeon. My servants let me down at their peril.' The stare became icy. 'You know that, don't you, Ichor?'

Ichor gulped and nodded quickly.

'Yes, Master,' he whispered. 'I do.'

Chapter Six

The hotel floorboards creaked under his feet as Joe made his way back along the corridor of the third floor. Turning the corner to climb the staircase up to his room, he came face to face with Anthonia. Her sudden appearance startled him and he jerked back with a gasp.

'Ah, sorry,' Joe blurted out. 'You gave me a fright.'

The girl showed no reaction but simply gazed at him for a second or two then said, 'Vampires.'

Joe was shocked to the soles of his shoes.

'P-pardon?' he stammered, hoping he hadn't heard right.

'Vampires,' repeated Anthonia, looking into his eyes with an intent expression on her face.

Joe's thoughts raced. *Who was this girl? What did she know? Had she seen Muesli and Corpus, was that it?* No, he told himself, surely not. No one had seen them. Vaguely he realized that she was talking again.

'There are meant to be vampires in the mountains,' she was saying. 'Have you heard those stories? Stories of a hidden place where the last vampires lurk? Have you?'

Joe managed a weak smile. 'Can't believe everything you hear, can you?' he replied. 'They're only stories after all.'

'Are they, though?' responded Anthonia slowly. She leant back against the wall and folded her arms, the light from the small stair window falling on her dark hair and pale face. 'Has it never occurred to you that the stories might be true?' She looked at Joe steadily and, without giving him a chance to reply, went on.

'Why did your dad say you weren't going into the mountains when you are?'

Once again Joe was startled.

'Wh-what do you mean?' he said quickly, his heart beginning to beat fast.

Anthonia shrugged.

'I was outside the door. I heard a bit of your dad's phone conversation. He said he was taking *them* to the mountain.'

Joe felt a surge of alarm but at the same time he was annoyed. So what if his dad had not told her the truth? It was really nothing to do with her.

'I don't think that's any of your business,' he replied hotly. 'You shouldn't go around listening at doors.' He stepped forward towards the foot of the stairs, intending to go to his room, but found himself stopped by Anthonia's outstretched hand.

'Wait a moment,' she said. 'Look, I'm sorry. It's just that . . .' She trailed off, then carried on fiercely. 'It's important, you see. Very important. I have to find out as much as I can. My information so far has come from research into local legend. All hearsay. Nobody I've spoken to has had any experience of vampires.'

Joe did what he thought was appropriate after such a remark. He snorted as if the very idea of meeting a vampire was nonsensical. 'Obviously,' he retorted, trying to make the word sound as scornful as possible, 'everyone knows vampires aren't real.' Anthonia didn't reply so Joe took his chance and hurried past her on to the stairs. 'Goodnight,' he said over his shoulder.

He was almost at the top when Anthonia spoke again.

'But they *are* real,' she said quietly.

Joe stopped and looked down at her pale, upturned face.

'How do you know?' he asked, his heart racing. Even from the top of the stairs Joe could see an intense, almost *mad* light dancing in her eyes again as she gazed up at him.

'From my great-grandmother,' she replied. There was a pause before she went on so softly that Joe had to strain to hear her words. 'She was a vampire hunter.'

Joe felt his jaw dropping in astonishment but could do nothing to stop it. He stood there, mouth agape, thoughts whirling as Anthonia, giving him one last look, turned and disappeared back along the corridor. Swallowing hard, Joe at last found his voice. 'Wait!' he croaked, and clattered down the stairs in pursuit. Reaching the bottom he ran into the corridor and slid to a halt on the polished floor. Anthonia had gone. In a panic, he rushed back upstairs to his room.

Vinny frowned when Joe told him what had happened.

'The girl's obviously got a big obsession,' he muttered. 'Her great-grandmother may well have been a vampire hunter but she's not around now, is she? No. Anthonia is just obsessed with her family's history, that's all. I don't think we should worry about it, Joe. She probably thought that we might have heard a story or two about vampires that she hadn't.' He glanced at his watch. 'Look, it's getting late. You get to bed and I'll go and have a word with Muesli and Corpus. Tell them to be extra watchful tonight.' He grinned mischievously. 'Just in case Anthonia takes her vampire-hunting too seriously and likes to wander around in the middle of the night with a hammer and a wooden stake.'

Joe winced.

'That's not funny, Dad.'

Vinny's smile grew broader.

'Of course it is, Joe. You don't actually think that Anthonia wants to follow in her great-grandmother's footsteps, do you?'

Chapter Seven

Little more than a walk-in cupboard, Anthonia's room was just big enough for a single bed and a tiny bedside table. Above the table a narrow window looked on to the town square. Anthonia's clothes were kept, neatly folded, in her suitcase, which lay open on the faded carpet at the foot of the bed. Her motorcycle crash helmet hung on the bedpost.

Anthonia sat on the bed. Spread out in front of her were the contents of her compact rucksack – a tattered sepia photograph, a small, worn, leather-backed diary, an old wide-brimmed hat trimmed with a leather band, a string of garlic bulbs, a small wooden crossbow, some slender oak darts, a tiny silver pistol and a few silver bullets. She stared at this strange collection for a little while then, as if coming out of a trance, took a deep breath and began to pack them away. Picking up the bullets, she put them into a small pouch and stored them in her rucksack. The pistol, crossbow and darts followed, with the string of garlic bulbs placed on top. Anthonia gazed at the sepia photograph for a long time. It showed a young woman in a tweed jacket, riding breeches, boots and a soft, wide-brimmed hat. Her long black hair was tied back, accentuating her pale face with its wide-set eyes and thick eyebrows. Laying the photograph carefully on the bed again, Anthonia picked up the diary and opened it at a marked page. She had read this entry many times but it never failed to affect her. She could hear her great-grandmother's voice in every line – could feel its strength, its anger – and could feel her own anger becoming stronger as she read.

The undead I have encountered in my travels have been, for the most part, pitiful creatures. Not in the sense of creating a

*feeling of pity in the onlooker but in the
sense of their wasted appearance. They are
hollow-cheeked and sunken-eyed, their long
eye teeth sharp but mottled and yellow.
I speak here of the poor denizens of the
graveyards and crypts, the rooftop crawlers
and alley-lurkers, not the sleek counts and
countesses in their mouldering castles.
Although not similar in appearance, the
poor vampires and the high-born vampires
have one thing in common. Both types are
merciless.*

A tap at the door made her close the book
quickly. Putting it into her rucksack she
pushed the old photograph under her pillow
and turned to face the door. 'Yes?'

'It's me,' called a light voice. Anthonia
lifted the rucksack and carefully slid it
and the hat out of sight underneath the
bed.

'Hold on,' she replied.

When Anthonia opened the door a
moment later, one of the first-floor maids
hurried in. Ellie, a year older than Anthonia,
was a small girl with blonde hair swept to
the top of her head and fastened with a
bright clasp.

Anthonia looked at Ellie's new dress and smiled.

'Nice.'

'Thanks,' Ellie said quickly and hurried on breathlessly. 'I wouldn't normally ask you but could you do me a favour? It's the end of my shift and my boyfriend's waiting. There are two bags of old curtains that need to go down to the bins to be picked up early tomorrow morning. They're dusty and I don't want to mark this dress. Could you take them down for me? Please?'

Anthonia nodded.

'Of course. I'll do it later.'

'Oh, you're a sweetie!' exclaimed Ellie. 'I owe you one.' Flashing Anthonia a grateful smile she rushed out.

Anthonia closed the door behind her and sat on the bed once more. Sliding her hand under the pillow she withdrew the sepia photograph of the young woman. She looked at it for a long time before lifting her eyes to the window to gaze out at the dark night sky.

Chapter Eight

'Can we go out now, Mooz? It's well after midnight.' Corpus looked hopefully at his friend and shifted uncomfortably on his bunk. 'I need to stretch, breathe some night air. I feel like a coiled spring.' He fiddled with the silver clasp on his cloak. 'I'll probably unwind and crash through the roof of this big sardine can.'

Muesli smiled and pulled up the collar of his high-buttoned black jacket. He knew how hard it was for his large friend to stay still for long. 'Let me just check again,' he replied.

The young vampire swivelled on his bunk, drew the edge of the blind away from the window slightly and peered out into the dark yard.

'All's well,' he said. 'The lights in all the rooms are out – everyone's in bed. I'll go first.' He slid from his bunk, padded the few steps to the door and quietly unlocked it. Inching it open he slid through and beckoned Corpus to follow.

With a broad smile the big vampire ducked through the doorway. Standing in the darkness between the caravan and the high wall, Corpus straightened to his full height and took a long, deep breath. He began to pad softly up and down in the narrow space, gulping in the cool air.

Count Muesli moved to the front of the caravan where a branch of the chestnut tree hung low. Through the leaves he could see the lamp shining above the hotel's back door, which left the rest of the building in darkness. Above the hotel, pale clouds drifted lazily across the dark sky, heading towards the distant mountains. Muesli's thoughts drifted with them – to Eyetooth. I wonder how my friends are faring? he thought. He sighed inwardly. The last few weeks had been hard for him, forced to hide in Joe's house while his broken arm mended, knowing that his friends were in danger. He wondered about Countess Alchema. Had she fully recovered from her terrible struggle with Fibula? Had her secret hiding place in her house been discovered? And what about Countess Bray? Would Fibula find out that she had helped Alchema escape? Had Krazul and Darceth managed to evade capture? He sighed again. There were others too who could be in danger. Grume, the one-legged owner of the Café in the Crypt whom Muesli and Corpus had freed from jail – and, of course, Corpus's assistant, Vane. Grume was hopefully well hidden in the passageways that ran underneath the Café in the Crypt but he wasn't sure about Vane. He hoped that the little werewolf hadn't come to any harm and that Fibula hadn't realized he was on their side.

A sudden, small noise from the hotel brought him back to the present and Muesli froze. He turned to Corpus who had amused himself by climbing up the face of the wall for a metre or so and was now moving crabwise towards him, a happy grin on his face. Muesli hissed urgently at the big vampire.

Corpus immediately dropped silently to

the ground and stayed in a crouch as his friend pointed at the back door of the hotel.

Turning again, Muesli was just in time to see the door opening and a girl with short dark hair emerge, carrying two large bags. He shrank back under the leaves and watched as she dropped the bags in the bin area at the side of the hotel. She turned round and Muesli retreated further into the shadow of the tree. The girl walked back towards the door but just as she got there she stopped, her hand on the knob. For a moment she just stood there, as if thinking – then, without warning, she turned on her heel and walked directly towards the caravan. Muesli spun round and, waving frantically to Corpus, ran to the door of the caravan and leapt lightly inside.

Corpus sprang after Muesli. Reaching out to grab the edge of the open door, he misjudged the distance and, instead of grasping it, knocked the door away from himself. It hit the side of the caravan with a sharp, tinny sound. Wincing, Corpus quickly seized it, pulled it shut behind him as quietly as he could and turned the key silently in the lock.

He and Muesli crouched inside, listening.

The girl's footsteps had stopped at the noise of the door hitting the caravan. There was a few seconds' silence then the two vampires heard her call out tentatively, 'Who's there?'

Not daring to move an inch the friends waited.

'Who's that?' came the voice again, and this time Muesli noticed that it was steady, unafraid.

Silence reigned again for a full thirty seconds before they heard her moving round the caravan, trying the windows and the door. 'Is there anyone in there?' she called quietly but firmly, twisting the door handle.

Muesli and Corpus hardly dared breathe. They stood as immobile as statues.

The girl moved round the caravan again, then when she reached the front once more, the two vampires heard her footsteps turn away from them and go in the direction of the hotel.

As quickly as he could, Muesli moved to the front window of the caravan. Stealthily he pulled back the edge of the blind and peered out. The girl had just reached the back door. Pausing there as she had done before, she turned slowly to look at the caravan. Muesli didn't move a muscle. After a moment the girl turned back to the door, opened it and went inside. A second later Muesli heard the faint sound of a key turning in the lock.

Chapter Nine

The early morning air was chilly and felt sharp as Joe crossed the yard towards the caravan. Vinny was still soundly asleep – along, it seemed, with the rest of the hotel. The only sound came from the whispering wind that carried the scent of mountain pine and damp bracken.

Muesli and Corpus were lying on their bunks but sat up when Joe came in.

'Everything all right?' Joe asked.

A few minutes later Joe had heard all about the mysterious girl who had taken such an interest in the caravan after midnight. Recognizing her from Muesli's description, he breathlessly related his own encounter with Anthonia to his amazed friends.

'I wonder how much she knows about vampires,' Muesli murmured.

'I don't know but Dad says she thinks we've got something to hide,' Joe replied.

Corpus chuckled. 'She's right. You have got something to hide. Us. And I nearly spoilt it all last night.'

'Don't worry about it, Corpy,' said Muesli. 'She didn't see us. She probably put the noise down to a cat or a rat.'

Corpus couldn't help himself. At the mention of the word *rat* he licked his lips.

Muesli grinned. 'We'll be back in Eye-tooth soon,' he said to his big friend. 'You can drink your fill of rats' blood then.'

'You'll both be OK until we leave?' Joe asked anxiously. 'It'll be sometime this afternoon, probably – the mechanic said he'd have the clutch cable fixed by then.'

Muesli nodded.

'We'll be all right.'

Corpus nodded too. 'Of course we will,' he said, and lay back on the bunk, his knees bent to allow himself to fit into the tiny space. 'But I have to say I'm looking forward to being able to stretch out to my proper length in my nice, comfortable coffin.'

Chapter Ten

After breakfast Joe and his dad packed their bags. As they were about to leave, a maid arrived at the door with fresh laundry. Joe was surprised to see it wasn't Anthonia but a small girl with wispy blonde hair who smiled at them cheerfully.

'Hi,' said the girl. 'All right if I do the room now?'

'Of course,' replied Vinny, then added, 'but where's the other girl – Anthonia? I thought she was the one who worked up here.'

'She does,' replied the maid, 'but she's taking a couple of days off work so I'm filling in for her. I think she said she was going out of town.'

'Ah, right,' said Vinny. 'Thanks.'

On the way downstairs Vinny chuckled.

'Well, at least Anthonia won't be hanging around today, Joe,' he said. 'I won't have to answer any more questions or tell any more fibs.'

Joe smiled.

'I know, Dad. I'm glad she's gone.'

As it was still only mid-morning, they left the bags behind the desk at reception and went for a stroll around the town. The film bug was beginning to nibble at Vinny by now and he was eager to see Muesli and Corpus off safely then return to the festival. He registered at the town hall and got a participants' information pack about all the films that were competing. Holding the pack up like a trophy and beaming broadly, Vinny suggested that they stop at a little pavement café while he read it. When they were settled at a table with coffee and orange juice Vinny took the brochure out of its envelope.

'Aha, here we are!' he crowed as he flipped through to the page that contained his own entry. 'Look what it says! "*It's not often we have a biting comedy worthy of the name, so it's refreshing to have one at this year's festival.* Vampires On Holiday *is a darkly atmospheric and very funny take on Hollywood's obsession with the undead. From first-time director, Vinny Price.*"' He beamed proudly at Joe. 'Not bad, eh?'

'Great, Dad!' Joe enthused. He looked at the accompanying still from the film and grinned broadly. 'Ha! There's Mum and Granny Roz as Count Clot's vampire aunts. They look fabulous. I remember the day we shot that scene.'

'Mum hated herself in the film,' Vinny chortled, 'but your gran loved it. She wants to be a star!'

'I can see Granny Roz at the Oscars, Dad, can't you?'

Vinny grinned.

'Of course I can. As long as I'm there too!'

They stayed at the café and had lunch. The town square was thronged now – tourists, film-makers and locals all enjoying themselves in the warm sunshine.

This would be just like a holiday, thought Joe, if it wasn't for Muesli and Corpus. What's going to happen to them when they get back? Will they be able to defeat Fibula?

He sighed inwardly. He wished his vampire friends didn't have to leave.

Vinny's mobile rang and he picked it up from the table.

It was Joe's mum, Nerys, phoning to see how things were going. Vinny explained about the delay.

'So you think Muesli and Corpus will be back in Eyetooth this evening?' she asked.

'Definitely,' responded Vinny.

'That's great,' said Nerys. 'Drive safely. By the way, here's Roz . . . she wants a word.'

'Don't you dare think of going up to Eyetooth with them, Vinny, my lad,' warned Roz when she came on the line.

'Of course not,' replied Vinny. 'That's not the plan.'

'Plans can change,' retorted Roz darkly.

Vinny grinned at Joe when at last he put the phone down.

'Your granny's just jealous that we're here and she's not.'

Joe laughed. 'I know. I think Granny Roz has been dreaming about giving Fibula a black eye!'

Chapter Eleven

The big oak door of Eyetooth's jail opened slowly. Vane's furry face peered out and looked up into the afternoon sky.

Shreds of misty cloud drifted slowly overhead and, although there was no hint of rain, Vane unfurled his torn old umbrella and hoisted it above his head. Somewhere in Vane's distant past – during the time when he was still a human and the change to being a werewolf had not occurred – he had almost drowned when he fell into a stream during a torrential downpour. Since that time he had developed a great fear of rain and never went outside without the protection of an umbrella over his furry head.

Pulling up the collar of his tattered tail-coat, Vane scurried across the empty square and into an ancient, winding street. In the silent, castellated houses on either side, vampires slept in their dark coffins or beds of fragrant earth. Creatures of the night, most vampires did not stir until twilight.

Count Fibula, however, was already awake. The fearsome leader of the vampire council slept only from dawn till midday and he was the one who had sent for the little werewolf.

Fibula had never called for him before and Vane was worried. Did the leader suspect that his sympathies lay with the rebels? Vane had gone quietly about his job as caretaker at the jail, so hoped that Fibula didn't know whose side he was on.

Vane's frown deepened. Some of Muesli's friends had been roughly handled by Spitz and Horba, Fibula's cruel 'chiefs of police'. The jail was now almost full of Fibula's supposed enemies, a few of them even chained to the walls of their cells. Vane sighed. He missed his old boss, Corpus, and

47

wondered how he was – Muesli too. Muesli and Corpus had always been kind to him. He wondered where they were now and if they would ever come back. There were a few things he could tell the big policeman about Fibula's plans. Vane's ears were sharp and he had overheard a number of secrets.

Only a few days ago he had warned the rebels that Fibula had found out about one of their meetings in the tunnels. So at the last moment the rebels changed their meeting place and left Fibula's men to wander and get lost in the maze of underground passages.

A new meeting was organized for tomorrow and so far Vane thought Fibula didn't know about it. Vane was as certain as he could be that he was not suspected of being a spy. So why did Fibula want to see him?

Troubled, he turned in through the gateway to Fibula's castle, crossed the misty courtyard and knocked on the castle door. He was ushered into a gloomy hallway by Ichor, and the little werewolf felt an instant chill in the air. Walking into Fibula's castle was like walking into a cold, underground cellar. He shivered as he glanced around at the broad, grey marble staircase that swept upwards into the shadows, at the heavy blood-red drapes and tall ornate doors – everything covered in decades of dust and cobwebs. Vane nervously followed Ichor, rolling up his umbrella as he went.

Count Fibula was seated at the far end of a long table in the centre of his great hall. Meagre flames from a pair of burning logs in the grate were the only source of light.

Fibula himself seemed to be part of the darkness – seemed to grow out of the shadows. As Vane approached he lifted a bony hand and pointed to the high-backed chair at the opposite end of the table.

'Sit,' he commanded in a rasping voice.

As the chair was low and Vane was short, the little werewolf's head and shoulders were the only parts of him visible above the top of the table. He peered anxiously along the table's dark length towards the narrow, cruel face at the other end.

Vane waited with bated breath for Fibula to speak.

There was a long moment of silence and then Fibula said, 'Rats, Vane?'

'I'm . . . I'm sorry?' replied Vane, startled.

'Rats,' said Fibula in a clearer tone. 'I believe you know about rats.'

Vane blinked. He did know about rats – he was a good judge of rodents. Corpus had always relied on Vane's choice of the best rats available.

He nodded and cleared his throat.

'Yes, that is true.'

Count Fibula's eyes glittered.

'I, on the other hand, know little of the creatures. But then again, each to his own.' His eyes narrowed. 'It seems that an unfortunate thing has happened. My supplier of rats has become . . . *indisposed*.' Fibula's lips twitched in a ghost of a smile and Vane heard Ichor shift uneasily behind him. 'He was consorting with the wrong types so had to be . . . locked up.' He leant forward slightly. 'This means that I no longer have a supplier. This is where you come in.'

On the one hand Vane was relieved – but on the other hand his heart sank because he knew what was coming next.

'You know where the *Rattery* is, don't you?' murmured Fibula.

The Rattery was a place where rats were bred. Its location deep in the tunnels was known only to a few and its secret jealously guarded. There weren't many ways to earn money on Eyetooth but breeding rats was one of them. Many vampires caught the rats that infested their own cellars and happily drank the blood but many had no access to rats at all.

Fibula's castle had no cellars or dungeons. They had been bricked up by the castle's previous owner, Countess Bray.

Vane swallowed nervously.

'I cannot reveal the whereabouts of the Rattery to you, Count Fibula,' he said hoarsely. 'I am sworn to secrecy.'

Fibula's expression remained impassive.

'I know that,' he replied. 'I could . . . *extract* . . . the location from you, no doubt, but this would take time. No, I do not require you to reveal the Rattery's location – I only require you to go there and obtain some prime rats for me.' His thin, dark lips tightened in a chilling smile. 'You see, Vane, *you* have the honour of becoming my new supplier.'

Vane gulped.

This was an honour he could do without.

Chapter Twelve

'Wake up, Joe,' Vinny said. 'Nearly there.'

Joe blinked in surprise and looked outside. He saw that they were just turning off the road into an overgrown track between thickets of trees. It was beginning to get dark and Vinny had switched on the headlights.

'I've been asleep!'

Vinny smiled.

'For nearly an hour. You obviously needed it. You were up early this morning.'

Hearing the buzz of an engine, Joe twisted round and saw a red and black motorbike sweep past on the narrow mountain road.

'That's probably the biker that I've been seeing on and off for the last hour or so,'

Vinny commented, glancing in his rear-view mirror. 'Maybe works at one of the outlying farms.' He drove on into the gathering dusk, the caravan bumping and swaying behind them. After ten minutes of following the turns and twists of the gradually narrowing track, Vinny said, 'I'll stop soon, Joe. It's safe now to let Muesli and Corpus sit in the car with us. And anyway,' he went on, peering ahead intently, 'they'll know where to turn off this path.' He glanced at the roughly drawn map that Muesli had made and which he had taped to the dashboard. 'I've been sure enough up until now but I think it's time to let the experts take over.'

A few minutes later Vinny stopped the car and Joe got out. As he closed the door he stood for a moment on the over-grown track and listened, frowning. They were miles from anywhere but he was sure he had just heard a faint engine noise. Now there was nothing – only the soft sighing of the evening breeze in the branches, and the cawing of far-off crows. He shrugged. The sound must have drifted on the wind from a remote farm somewhere.

The two vampires were delighted to be

able to leave the confines of the caravan at last. They got into the car eagerly, Muesli sitting beside Vinny while Joe and a beaming Corpus sat in the back, both craning forward to see where they were going. Muesli directed Vinny, showing him how the forest paths corresponded to his lines on the map. He told them about the secret entrance, describing its appearance and how it was virtually invisible to those who did not know what to look for.

'Directly above it is a rock shaped like a jagged thorn,' said Muesli.

'Can we drive right up to it, Muesli?' asked Joe.

'No, Joe,' replied Muesli. 'The undergrowth is too thick.' He stared fixedly at the narrow track ahead, illuminated by the headlights, then suddenly pointed to a gnarled willow whose branches drooped low. The venerable tree was almost hidden in the thick undergrowth but on one side its lower branches curved to form a dark opening. 'That is where we'll leave you,' he said. 'The hidden entrance to the tunnel that leads through the mountain to Eyetooth is not far from here in a direct line due east.' The car stopped by the tree and Muesli glanced at Vinny. 'There is a small clearing just ahead where you will be able to turn the car and caravan round.' Out on the darkening track the four of them stood around awkwardly, no one knowing how to begin to say goodbye now that the moment had come.

Joe took a deep breath and held out his hand to Muesli.

'It's been so great knowing you,' he said, shaking the young vampire's hand, then Corpus's. 'Both of you. I'll never forget you.'

Vinny shook the vampires by the hand too.

'I wish you all the luck in the world,' he said with feeling. 'Give our regards to Countess Alchema.'

'And Countess Bray,' added Joe, his voice anxious. 'I hope all of your friends are OK – and I hope . . . I hope Fibula gets what he deserves.'

'Thank you both,' Muesli replied. 'It has been a privilege for two vampires to have met with such understanding and friendliness from outsiders. I will always remember it.'

'I will too,' said Corpus. 'I'll also

remember your bravery when you helped us escape from Fibula's cell in Eyetooth, Joe.'

'Well said, Corpy,' added Muesli, smiling at Joe. 'We owe you a lot, Joe.'

Joe smiled self-consciously, lost for words.

Corpus swept his cloak back across both shoulders and was clearly eager to be off.

'Good luck to you both and to your family,' he said, then looked at his companion. 'It's time to go, Mooz.'

'Yes,' Muesli answered. 'It is time.' He and Corpus bowed formally to Joe and Vinny, then turning abruptly, they disappeared from sight under the branches of the willow.

Joe felt a lump rise in his throat and clenched his fists tightly. He and Vinny stood looking into the darkness under the willow branches.

Vinny sighed. 'Come on, Joe,' he said quietly. 'We should be getting back.'

Chapter Thirteen

Corpus forged ahead, pushing the dense forest aside with ease, cracking large branches underfoot as if they were twigs. Eventually, pulling back the thick and thorny undergrowth, he finally encountered the smooth surface of the rock face. He and Muesli slid into the dank space between the bushes and the cliff and, looking up, saw the distinctive thorn-shaped spur directly above them. Springing on to the sheer rock face, the two vampires swarmed effortlessly upwards and, moments later, reached a narrow ledge that jutted out in front of the hidden entrance. Without looking back they squeezed through the opening, crouching low to prevent themselves from cracking their heads against the tunnel roof. After a few metres they were able to straighten up and Corpus turned to Muesli with a grin, his sharp white teeth glinting in the darkness. 'Don't know what's in store for us,' he whispered, 'but it's wonderful to be going home, isn't it?'

Muesli smiled too, a fierce light dancing in his eyes. 'It is,' he agreed. 'Fibula has a surprise coming.'

Chapter Fourteen

Anthonia easily followed the noisy progress of Muesli and Corpus through the under-growth – despite the muffled sound of the car engine far behind her. Her tiredness after hours of playing cat and mouse with the car and caravan had vanished. She felt strong, excited.

Her decision to follow Joe and his father from the hotel had been based purely on instinct – on the feeling that in some strange way there was a *connection* between them and herself. Also . . . she was sure they were hiding something – *or someone*.

It had taken a lot of skill and nerve to follow them into the forest. From her hiding place she had seen figures emerge from the caravan – *two figures in flowing black cloaks* – one huge, with tangled black hair, the other slim and pale, with a shock of orange hair. Even now, as she crept through the forest after them, her heart leapt. The stories about this mountain had been true after all – *the cloaked figures were vampires!* The boy and his father were obviously in league with them and had helped the vampires return to their lair. Another little electric shiver of excitement crackled through her body and she smiled grimly to herself. I will finish the work my great-grandmother began, she thought. I will fulfil my destiny!

Ahead, the noise of the two vampires' progress suddenly stopped. Anthonia hesitated, listening intently. She craned forward and, looking up through the leaves, saw two dark shapes moving up the rock face. As she watched, the figures suddenly disappeared. Lunging forward, ignoring the thorns and twigs that snagged her leather jacket and trousers, she soon found the surface of the rock face.

The light was fading fast now but Anthonia did not want to risk using her torch. Peering upwards into the gloom she searched the face of the steep rock where she had last seen the figures. Making sure her backpack straps were tight she began climbing. It was difficult but Anthonia was nimble and light, with strong fingers and legs, and she soon found herself standing on a narrow ledge. Catching her breath there in the growing darkness, she saw that the ledge jutted out from a hidden cleft in the rock face. This was where they had gone! Quickly she moved across the ledge and shone her torch into the black space. A low tunnel stretched away from her and up into the darkness. Anthonia took a long, slow breath and, crouching, started to climb the rocky slope.

Chapter Fifteen

With little room to manoeuvre, it had been tricky to turn the car and caravan round in the clearing but Vinny had done it. At last they were driving slowly back the way they had come, their headlights illuminating the undergrowth, making the green leaves appear white.

Joe watched the old willow approach and took one last, regretful look at the tree where Muesli and Corpus had vanished into the tangle of vegetation. Suddenly he leant forward and stared into the confusion of leaves and branches.

'Dad! Stop!'

Startled, Vinny braked.

'What's up, Joe?'

But Joe was already out of the car and bounding away.

Vinny saw his son disappear into the undergrowth just beyond the caravan.

'Joe!' he cried. 'What on earth –?' He ran round the car and met Joe as he re-emerged. Vinny saw there was an excited look on his son's face. 'What is it?'

'In there, Dad!' Joe gasped. 'The headlights caught something that flashed like silver as we went past!'

Vinny bent low and peered into the dark space under the tangle of branches and tendrils. It took a second for his eyes to adjust to the gloomy greenness but then he saw it. His eyes widened and he backed out and stood up straight, scratching his head.

'A motorbike,' he said, amazed.

'Not just any motorbike, Dad,' replied Joe. 'It's the one that passed us on the road a while back. I recognize the black and red panniers.'

Vinny frowned.

'Has he been following us? The biker must be around somewhere.'

Joe grabbed his father's arm.

'Dad! I've seen that bike before! In the car

park at the back of the hotel!' Vinny's eyes widened in shock as a thought struck him. 'Surely you don't think it's . . .?'

Joe nodded agitatedly.

'Yes, yes! It has to be her, Dad. Vampire-obsessed Anthonia. Got to be. She's followed us here wondering what we're up to. *She must've seen Muesli and Corpus.*'

Vinny whistled softly under his breath. 'We have to go get her, Dad! If she follows Muesli and Corpus into the mountain she could be attacked by vampires. She's in real danger. She might even try to harm our friends!' He turned and ran to the nearby willow where Muesli and Corpus had disappeared. 'Come on,' he cried. 'We have to go.'

Vinny wasn't sure. He looked anxiously towards the mountain and raised his hands to his mouth.

'Anthonia! Anthonia!'

There was no reply.

'She's too far ahead of us, Dad,' said Joe. 'She won't hear. It took you a while to turn the car round. And even if she did hear you I don't think she'd answer. She doesn't know what she's getting herself into.'

'Right, yes, well . . .' Vinny turned

64

towards the car, turned back towards Joe then back towards the car again. 'I . . . er . . . no . . . you're right. We have to go after her. We've got no choice.' He made a face. 'I can imagine what your mother – and your Granny Roz – would say about this. But a phone call would just worry them.' He hurried to the car, keys in hand. 'I'll get a torch and lock the car.'

'Come on, Dad!' exclaimed Joe, hopping about anxiously.

His father ran back towards him carrying their jackets and a torch, a determined expression on his face.

'Let's go,' said Vinny purposefully.

Together they ducked beneath the branches of the old willow and plunged into the night-dark greenery.

It was hard going – the underbrush so dense that sometimes they had to make detours round the thicker masses of bush and briar. Eventually Vinny unscrewed the detachable compass in the base of the torch and directed the beam on to it. He nodded in satisfaction.

'We're OK. Still going in the right direction – due east, Muesli said.' He replaced the compass and flashed the torchlight ahead of them. 'This way.' He set off again, brushing tall ferns and bristling leaves aside.

Joe followed directly behind him, trying his best to avoid the branches that sprang back from his dad's charging progress. He kept as close as he could to his father, watching his feet in case he tripped on a low branch or got snagged on a thorny creeper. Suddenly Vinny stopped.

'Ah!' he grunted. 'We have contact.'

'What, Dad?'

'Feels like the wall of rock,' responded Vinny, moving forward through a thick tangle of creepers.

Joe squirmed his way through after his dad and found himself in a narrow, dank space between the vegetation and a precipitous rock face.

Vinny played his torch back and forth along the stony surface.

'So, where's the tunnel entrance?' he muttered anxiously.

Joe craned his neck and scanned the rocks above him.

'A rock shaped like a thorn, Muesli said. Can't see anything.' He looked to his left and then to his right along the narrow passageway between the forest and the rock face. 'Could be either way.'

'Let's try right,' said Vinny. He moved off slowly, playing the torch beam over the rock surface above him. Behind him Joe gazed upwards, searching for the telltale rock.

After a minute Vinny groaned and shook his head in exasperation. 'No . . . no . . . nothing,' he murmured. 'It's like looking for a needle in a –'

'Wait, Dad,' cried Joe suddenly. 'Move the light back a bit!'

The beam of light rippled along the surface, showing up the dents and indentations in the seemingly sheer rock.

'There!'

Ahead of them, about four or five metres from the ground, a curved and pointed spur of rock jutted upwards into the gathering darkness.

'Yes. I see it. I'll light your way, Joe,' said Vinny. 'When you get up there I'll throw you the torch.'

'OK, Dad.'

Vinny shone his torch on the rock and Joe started climbing, instinctively finding hand and footholds as he clambered up eagerly.

When he reached the ledge Vinny carefully threw the torch to him. Following the bright pool of light that Joe directed down the rock face, Vinny climbed slowly, grunting with effort, and at last dragged himself, panting, on to the stone ledge.

'This is it, Dad,' Joe said tensely, shining the torch into the hidden cleft. 'There's a tunnel here that goes up into the mountain.'

The mobile in Vinny's jacket pocket suddenly rang and, startled, Vinny stepped back, one foot slipping over the edge. A clatter of small stones cascaded down the rock face as he staggered, trying to keep his balance.

Frantically Joe lunged forward, grabbed his dad's arm and managed to pull him to safety against the rocky wall.

'Phew!' Vinny gasped as he leant back gratefully. 'Thanks, Joe! Close call.'

Joe smiled and made a wry face.

'Close *call*? Good joke, Dad!'

'Hah hah,' said Vinny, taking out his phone. 'Hello, Roz,' he began, then grimaced at Joe. 'Terrible reception. Hello . . . hello?' He listened for a moment longer, shrugged and disconnected. 'Could hardly hear her.' He shook his head ruefully. 'Your granny certainly has a knack for ringing at the wrong time.' He looked sideways at the hidden entrance. 'Mind you, once inside the mountain there'll be no signal at all.'

'Maybe just as well, Dad,' replied Joe with a grin.

Vinny chortled and took a deep breath. 'Right, Joe. Let's go.'

They stepped inside the entrance. But after only a few paces Joe tapped his dad on the arm and Vinny stopped.

'Maybe we should shout again, Dad,' he said. 'We've got to try and stop Anthonia. If she's chasing Muesli and Corpus she won't answer but at least she'll know we're coming after her.'

Vinny nodded then abruptly changed his nod into a shake of the head.

'Maybe not such a good idea, Joe. What if one of Fibula's vampires is lurking in the tunnels and hears us?'

Joe frowned.

'You're right, Dad. Better to be quiet.'

'I think so,' replied Vinny. He took another deep breath.

So did Joe, feeling a small shiver of fear prickle the hairs on the back of his neck as they moved deeper into the tunnel, and the comforting shape of the entrance was lost to view.

Chapter Sixteen

Muesli and Corpus sped through the utter blackness, their fingers lightly tracing the cold outlines of the smooth rock walls of the rising tunnel. Despite the darkness they found it easy to see here – their vision helped by the billions of tiny crystals in the rock that gave off microscopic amounts of light. To the vampires' keen eyes it was almost like walking on a moonless, starlit night with the faint shapes of the constellations all around them. The two friends had been moving steadily upwards for almost an hour, easily finding their way through the underground maze. Twice the tunnels had broadened out into enormous, dripping caverns, created in prehistoric times by erosion and volcanic action. The caverns' floors and ceilings were connected by hundreds of natural stone pillars and it was in these places, centuries before, that vampires had begun work on underground palaces. The stone pillars were carved to resemble foliage-covered columns – capitals, lost in the arcing blackness, were hewn into the shapes of mythical beasts and birds of prey. Sculpted gargoyles and coats of arms decorated the dark walls. Work had never been completed on these underworld palaces and now they survived as long-empty follies, hidden away in the heart of the mountain of Eyetooth.

Muesli suddenly stopped and drew Corpus into the recess of a deep alcove.

'Shh,' he whispered into his friend's ear. 'Someone's coming.' He and Corpus stood quite still, listening intently. After a moment they became aware of a low muttering noise and what sounded like the patter of small feet. A faint glow of light came closer.

Muesli heard Corpus catch his breath in surprise then chuckle softly.

The big vampire moved forward quietly,

then suddenly reached out, grasped hold of the small figure that had appeared and pulled it into the alcove.

The figure gasped in fright, rearing back and staring upwards, its umbrella raised to strike.

'It's all right, Vane,' hissed Corpus in delight. '*It's me.*'

The little werewolf stared in astonishment at the huge shape towering over him, then slowly lowered his battered brolly and hooked it over his arm.

'Count ... Corpus ...?' he croaked hoarsely, holding up his little lantern so that it shone on the vampires' faces. 'Can it really be you?' He looked wildly from Corpus to Muesli. 'You too!'

Corpus beamed. 'My goodness ...' he began but Vane suddenly shot out a small furry hand and clapped it over his surprised former boss's mouth, gesturing desperately over his shoulder with his other hand. He then beckoned Corpus and Muesli to come close.

'We must be quiet,' he hissed, barely audible. 'I'm being followed. Think it might be Ichor. Let me try and lose him and then I'll come back.' He put a finger to his lips and motioned for them to go deeper into the alcove.

Vane turned, peered out into the gloom and carried on his way as if nothing had happened, muttering to himself and scuffling his feet. As the sound of his progress faded away along with the light of his lantern Muesli and Corpus became aware of another sound – that of someone moving stealthily but not as stealthily as a vampire. They waited silently and after a few moments a short, squat shape appeared and moved across the mouth of the alcove, intent on following Vane but unaware of the two watchers.

Corpus and Muesli shared a quick glance of recognition.

The figure moved out of sight and the two friends waited without speaking until Vane padded into the alcove beside them again.

'Lost him,' he said with satisfaction as he relit his lantern. 'It was Ichor right enough. He'll be wandering around for hours before he finds his way out.'

He looked up at the two vampires, his eyes twinkling, a wide grin of delight on his face.

'I still can't believe it,' he whispered. 'You two . . . back again.'

'Our human friends brought us as far as the forest,' Corpus explained, beaming. 'It's good to see you, Vane,' he went on warmly, patting the little werewolf on the shoulder.

'It certainly is,' agreed Muesli. 'And good to see you are still able to go about your business. Where are you off to, by the way?'

Vane's smile faded.

'The Rattery,' he replied. 'Fibula found out that I know its location. His supplier of rats is in prison so he ordered me to fetch him some. Rats, that is. I was on my way when I realized I was being followed by Ichor. I caught a glimpse of him just before I entered the tunnels. Fibula obviously sent him after me. He wants to find out where the Rattery is. He hates the fact that there are things in Eyetooth that he doesn't know about.'

'How *are* things in Eyetooth?' asked Muesli with concern.

The little werewolf grimaced.

'Not good, Count Muesli,' he replied. 'Fibula has Eyetooth in an iron grip. He has recruited more policemen who go around in patrols making sure the curfew is heeded.

Anyone caught out after eight o'clock at night is assumed to be an enemy and thrown into prison.'

Corpus frowned angrily at the mention of policemen. 'A month ago I was the only policeman that Eyetooth needed,' he growled.

'Who is in prison, Vane?' asked Muesli.

'Anyone that Fibula doesn't like.' Vane shook his head mournfully. 'Many of your friends. Although he still hasn't caught Countess Alchema or Countess Bray,' he added. 'And Krazul and Darceth, and their sister, are still at liberty.'

'That at least is good news,' replied Muesli fervently. 'But what about Fibula's plans to send vampires out into the world again? Has he done it? Are we too late to stop it?'

'No,' replied Vane quickly. 'He hasn't done that yet. But there are six vampires close to him who are hungry for human blood.' He fingered his brolly nervously. 'A nasty lot. From what I can gather, they'll be leaving Eyetooth soon.'

'How soon?' Muesli stared intently at the little werewolf.

'Could be in the next few days,' said

Vane. 'Once Fibula has silenced all opposition. I was going to tell Alchema about it but had to come here first.' He looked with concern at his friends. 'What are you going to do?'

'Find Alchema and the others,' responded Muesli grimly. 'Fibula has to be stopped. Those vampires must not leave Eyetooth.'

'One minute with that weasel,' Corpus said, cracking his knuckles and scowling. 'That's all I need. Just one.'

'I'm still employed at the jail, Count Corpus,' said Vane. 'Just as a caretaker now. But I've been able to pick up useful bits of information there – and pass them on.'

'Well done, Vane,' said Corpus approvingly. 'Very well done. When I'm Eyetooth's policeman again I'll promote you to Special Constable.' He patted the little werewolf's shoulder. 'You're a good friend.'

Vane looked pleased and shuffled his feet bashfully.

'Ah, good. Right then,' he mumbled, lifting up his lantern. 'Good luck to you both.' Holding his tattered umbrella out in front of him like a sword, the little werewolf turned and trotted off into the darkness.

Muesli and Corpus watched the bobbing light from the lantern become fainter and fainter until it finally disappeared.

Chapter Seventeen

Joe and Vinny moved steadily up the tunnel, listening intently for any sound that might tell them where Anthonia was. Overhead, smooth walls curved, broken only occasionally by deep niches and narrow cracks. Every so often they passed an ancient iron torch bracket bolted high on the walls. Some still had the stumps of centuries-old candles in them. Vinny took a couple of these and put them in his pocket in case the torch failed. The pathway twisted and turned, rising all the time, and after climbing for what seemed like an age, Joe and Vinny found themselves in a huge, open space. Immense stone columns sprang upwards into the blackness like a plantation of gigantic beanstalks, stretching away into the gloom beyond the torchlight. The only sound in the cavern was the soft, echoey *plop plop* of dripping water that oozed from the blackness above their heads to fall to the stony floor.

'It's like an enormous forest of stone,' breathed Joe as he and his father walked among the pillars. 'Fantastic.'

'It's incredible, Joe,' murmured Vinny, overwhelmed. 'Like a wonder of the world.'

Joe shone the torch over the columns.

'Which way, Dad?'

Vinny pointed towards a gap between the stone pillars.

'That way,' he said firmly. 'The columns are further apart there. It looks like an avenue that's been deliberately cut through a forest. It runs directly away from the tunnel we came out of, so let's follow it. Fingers crossed it will lead us to another tunnel on the opposite side.'

They set off, keeping to the centre of the pillared avenue, both keenly aware of the huge space that stretched away on all sides into the darkness.

Vinny stopped abruptly. 'Hold on . . . what's this?'

In the light of the torch they saw two huge statues – great winged beasts – standing as if on guard in the centre of the avenue. Their fangs bared, their bat-like wings spread, the two stone creatures reared up, frozen forever in the act of leaping into the air.

Joe gasped in admiration. 'Cool,' he said. As he and his dad approached Joe realized that the statues marked the beginning of a bridge that arched over a wide, black chasm.

Vinny took the torch and began edging forward.

Joe hung back. For all his efforts to be brave he still had a fear of heights.

'Don't get too close, Dad.'

'Don't worry, Joe. Just want to see what's what here.' Vinny shone the light over the brink and whistled softly. 'Deep,' he said as the probing torch beam failed to find the bottom. 'Looks like it runs the whole width of this place.' He joined Joe by the statues and they both peered over the bridge. 'Should we cross, do you think?'

'But is it safe, Dad?' returned Joe.

'Probably . . .' Vinny began but got no further.

'No!' came an urgent whisper from the darkness.

Joe and Vinny recoiled in shock and swivelled towards the sound, Vinny's agitated torch beam casting crazy shadows between the giant stone pillars.

'Do not cross,' the insistent voice continued. 'Stay where you are.'

Joe stood tensed, not knowing what to expect, as his dad steadied the beam and pointed it at a nearby column.

'Who are you?' Vinny demanded with as much force as he could muster. 'Come on out! Show yourself!'

A small furry head slowly came into view from behind the column and Joe gasped in delight.

'Vane!'

Vinny was startled.

'What . . .?' He glanced quickly at his son then back at the tiny figure with its hairy face and pointed ears. 'You know this . . . *person*?'

'It's Vane, Dad,' cried Joe. 'Corpus's assistant.'

A slow smile spread on Vinny's face. 'Ah. Of course. Vane.'

The little werewolf emerged from his

hiding place into the light, wisps of smoke drifting upwards from his extinguished lantern. In his other hand he clutched his trusty brolly.

Joe rushed to meet him, grinning from ear to ear.

'Oh, it's so brilliant we've met you, Vane,' he said excitedly.

'I know all about you, of course,' Vinny said, relaxing now. 'From Corpus and Muesli. We couldn't have met a better person.'

'I saw your light from the other side of the palace,' Vane replied in a low, concerned voice. 'I wondered who it was.' He looked around furtively, then, fumbling in his jacket pocket, he removed a box of flints, struck one and relit his hooded lantern. 'Please put that torch out,' he urged quietly. 'It's too bright. It's not safe. We don't know who else is down here.'

Chapter Eighteen

Ichor's squat figure dodged from column to column, steadily drawing nearer to the small glow of light in the far reaches of the dripping stone forest. He was panting from his exertions and stopped for a moment to catch his breath, peering ahead through the rows of columns. You didn't give me the slip after all, Vane, he thought. You managed to slip past me in the dark but when you blew out the candle I followed the smoky smell. You can't fool Ichor so easily.

Cautiously he crept forward again, ignoring the soaking his feet were getting from the puddles and pools on the rocky floor, trying to get close enough without being seen. He was desperately curious to know what Vane was doing and eager for any information that he could take back to Fibula. As he neared the flickering light he began to pick up vague echoey sounds and wondered what they were. Could they be voices? Stopping again, he strained to hear but shook his head in annoyance, wishing for a vampire's sharp hearing. *He was too far away. He had to get closer.*

Chapter Nineteen

'Be seated.' Count Fibula gestured to the six high-backed chairs that had been placed along one side of the long, oaken table.

The group of vampires who had just entered Fibula's great hall sat and, as one, turned to face their leader.

Fibula gazed at them, satisfaction glimmering in his dark eyes.

'Excellent,' he said softly. 'You are the chosen ones. You will be remembered forever as the vanguard of a new vampire empire.' He stared briefly, keenly, at each one as he recited their names: 'Horba, Spitz, Scabrus, Crusst, Sleed, Blech.'

As their names were uttered each vampire

bowed his head in a gesture of acknowledge-
ment. Sharp teeth caught the candlelight
as they smiled their cold, greedy smiles
in anticipation of what they knew was to
come – not only the unlimited prospect of
plump, human necks but also, in a moment,
*their first taste of human blood for over half
a century.* Their leader had promised that
he would give them a little foretaste of their
intended prey. And, sure enough, there it
was in front of Fibula – an elegant, glittering
crystal decanter containing a small amount
of the precious dark-red liquid.

Fibula stretched out a bony hand and
grasped the neck of the decanter.

'This, I believe, used to belong to
Countess Plaza.' He paused, a cold smile
twitching at the corners of his mouth.
'Before it was ... *stolen* ... by Count
Muesli.'

A sniggering wave of laughter rippled
along the table. The other vampires knew
that Fibula's servant, Ichor, had stolen
the decanter on Fibula's orders so that
Muesli could be blamed and banished from
Eyetooth.

'The countess demanded its return in such
forceful terms that, alas, I had no option but

to jail her,' Fibula went on languidly, 'and, of course, no option but to confiscate all of her property.' He tapped his long, curved nails on the silver plaque engraved with the letter *P* that hung round the neck of the decanter, and glanced towards the door impatiently. 'It seems that Ichor has been delayed.' He remained staring at the door for a few seconds longer, impatiently drumming his fingers on the table, then fixed his gaze on the vampire nearest to him. 'On the cabinet behind you, Scabrus, you will find a tray. Bring it here.'

Scabrus rose immediately and went to the heavy, carved-oak cabinet that loomed in the shadows by the far wall, returning a moment later bearing a gleaming silver tray on which were seven very small wine glasses and a tiny spoon with a long, curving handle. He laid the tray on the table in front of his leader and resumed his seat.

Fibula picked up the spoon and regarded them with his reptilian stare.

'Tomorrow night you will find and capture my remaining enemies, which means you will be free to leave here in a few days as my emissaries. So, as promised, here is your first tiny sample of what you . . . and

I . . . will shortly have in plentiful supply . . . *human blood*.'

Removing the decanter's crystal stopper, Fibula dipped the spoon into the blood, watched eagerly by six pairs of glinting eyes. As he lifted it out and poured its minute and glistening contents into the first glass, Fibula sighed.

'Plaza's secret process has worked wonderfully,' he murmured. 'This blood must be a hundred years old but it looks . . .' he sniffed the glass, 'and *smells* . . . very fresh.' He glanced along the table at the expectant faces. 'I will make it a priority to . . . *extract* . . . the secret from the countess at the earliest opportunity.' Another ripple of cold laughter passed along the table as Fibula delivered exact and tiny amounts of blood to every glass.

'Distribute them,' Fibula intoned.

Scabrus placed a glass in front of Fibula, then placed one in front of each of the other vampires. He sat down again, gazing hungrily at the thimbleful of blood before him.

Round the table all eyes were fixed on the tiny glasses glimmering in the firelight. The vampires shifted in their seats and leant forward expectantly, their faded black silk cloaks pulled aside, their hands resting on the oak boards.

Fibula raised his glass and immediately the vampires raised their own, turning eager faces to their leader.

'To the creation of my vampire empire!' Fibula cried.

'The empire!' chorused the vampires.

As one, glasses were lifted to thin lips and the blood tipped into dark mouths. All eyes glazed in pleasure at the first, sweet taste, and seven purple, pointed tongues flicked into the drained glasses, each one searching out and greedily licking up the last drops of the red liquid that clung to the sides.

Chapter Twenty

'It is lucky I found you when I did and stopped you from crossing the bridge,' Vane whispered to Joe and Vinny. 'The centre is dangerously weak.' He peered up at them in concern. 'But what will you do now? What about this Anthonia you speak of?'

'Well,' answered Vinny quietly, 'we can't leave her here, that's for sure.'

A sudden, faint scuffling sound to their right startled them and, without thinking, Vinny clicked on the torch and swung the beam towards the noise. What they saw made them start in surprise.

Walking towards them along the edge of the abyss was a tall figure wearing black leather and a wide-brimmed hat. A small, silver gun was levelled at them.

'Anthonia!' gasped Joe.

'Switch off that torch!' The command was sharp.

Vinny switched it off and was immediately blinded by the light of Anthonia's own torch as she pointed it into their faces.

'We've been looking for you,' Vinny said, shielding his eyes and squinting to see past the glare. 'You shouldn't be here. And what on earth are you doing with that silly thing?' he demanded, frowning in annoyance and indicating the gun. 'It's dangerous to point a gun at anyone. Come on . . . put it away and we'll all leave together.'

'I won't be leaving until I have fulfilled my destiny.' Anthonia's voice appeared calm.

Joe began to walk towards her.

'Listen, Anthonia . . .' he began.

'Stop there!'

The pistol was now aimed at him, and Joe stopped abruptly, his heart racing. He'd never had a gun pointed at him before. It was really scary.

'Move aside.'

Joe falteringly took a step to his right.

'You . . . *thing* . . .' She flicked the torch

beam at Vane. '*Werewolf.* Move to the left.'

Joe glanced over his shoulder and saw Vane hesitate, a look of alarm on his furry face.

'For goodness' sake, Anthonia . . .' Vinny began to protest but Anthonia ignored him, glaring harder at Vane.

'Move!'

The werewolf reluctantly shuffled sideways and stood frowning, his little hairy hands clasping and unclasping the handle of his brolly.

Turning back to Anthonia, Joe was horrified to see her point the gun at the little werewolf.

'Who . . . Why are you here?' asked Vane in a tremulous voice.

'I am here to destroy your kind!' Anthonia whispered, a fierce excitement in her voice. Then suddenly she cried loudly, her voice icy.

'*I am a vampire hunter!*'

Chapter Twenty-one

Ichor was shocked. *Vampire hunter?* Was this possible? Confused, he backed away but unintentionally moved out of the shadows and was briefly illuminated in the beam from the vampire-hunter's torch. He ducked back frantically but there was a sudden, sharp *crack*, a spit of flame and Ichor gasped in terror as a bullet smacked into the carved foliage just above his head, sending fragments of stone flying all around him. Stumbling backwards, wide-eyed, he turned and ran for his life, one phrase repeating inside his head in time to the slap of his flying feet – *Vampire hunter, vampire hunter, vampire hunter . . . !*

Chapter Twenty-two

Joe leapt towards Anthonia frantically, shouting, 'Stop it!'

Desperately he seized Anthonia's arm as tightly as he could, trying to make her drop the gun.

The girl struggled wildly.

'No! Let . . . go!' she seethed. 'Let . . . me . . . go!'

Vinny hurled himself towards the grappling figures and took hold of Anthonia's wrists. The girl struggled even harder, twisting and writhing with such force that they tripped over each other's feet and all three tumbled to the ground.

Anthonia let out a yell of fury as her hand

struck the ancient paving and she dropped the pistol. The little silver gun skidded away from her and came to rest at Vane's feet.

Vinny grabbed the shoulders of Anthonia's biker jacket and managed to pin her to the ground while Joe scrambled to his feet.

'For goodness' sake, Anthonia!' cried Vinny angrily through gritted teeth. 'Calm down! You could have killed someone with that thing!'

Suddenly Anthonia stopped struggling and lay quietly, her right cheek pressed to the flagstones, eyes staring across the cold surface to the small silver object only two metres away from her face.

'That was the idea,' she hissed fiercely. 'Vampires and their like have to be killed!'

Vinny shook his head angrily. 'It's madness! You're not thinking straight!'

Vane looked down distastefully at the gun at his feet. He shook his head too.

'Silver gun. Silver bullets,' he murmured and shuddered. 'I have heard of such horrible things.' With a quick, sweeping movement of his foot he kicked the pistol to one side, sending it skidding across the paving.

Anthonia's eyes widened in panic as she saw the gun disappear over the edge of the chasm, its small silver barrel glinting in the light for the last time as it plunged out of sight into the impenetrable blackness below.

'No!' she cried angrily. 'No!'

Instinctively Vinny gripped the girl's shoulders more tightly, expecting an explosive struggle, but after her shout Anthonia became still again. Vinny felt her relax so he gradually let go and sat back on his haunches.

Crouched beside his dad, Joe saw that Anthonia had closed her eyes. He watched her for a few seconds then said, 'Anthonia . . . are you OK?'

Anthonia took a deep breath and then exhaled slowly. Opening her eyes, she looked up at him.

'Of course,' she replied, her expression calm.

Joe looked at her intently.

'Things are sometimes not what they seem, Anthonia,' he said. 'Vane is a werewolf, yes . . . but he's a friend. A good person. And not all werewolves are bad, you know. Same with vampires. Those two vampires you followed . . . they are friends too.' He leant closer and said earnestly, '*They saved my life . . . and my family's lives.*'

Anthonia stared at him in silence for a few moments, her eyes as dark and fathomless as the chasm.

'So . . .' she murmured at last, 'there *are* bad werewolves . . . and bad vampires.'

'Yes,' Joe said. 'But –'

'But that doesn't mean that you should hunt them,' Vinny interrupted. 'It's not your business, Anthonia. They have done nothing to you.' He frowned. 'Lucky you missed. Anyway, the bad vampires are best left to be dealt with by the good ones like Count Muesli and Count Corpus up in Eyetooth. They're trying to prevent the bad vampires going after humans again.'

At the mention of Eyetooth Anthonia's eyes glittered. 'I see,' she said. She looked at Vinny. 'I'm getting up now, OK?'

Vinny nodded and stood up.

'As long as you are not going to do anything foolish – like run away.'

'I won't run away.'

Joe stood up too and watched as Anthonia slowly got to her feet, picking up her hat, which had fallen off as she fell. Placing the hat back on her head and tying it firmly under her chin by the leather strap, she glanced at Vane, then back at Vinny. Her expression was hard to read.

'So, what now?' she said.

Before Vinny could reply a chilling cry tore the air.

'Take them!'

Shocked, all four of them jerked round towards the sound and were appalled to see four swirling black shapes bearing down on them from the darkness.

Chapter Twenty-three

Muesli and Corpus emerged from the tunnels on to one of the great spurs of rock that erupted round the vampire mountain retreat like huge, rotten teeth.

The two friends were hidden from any prying eyes for the moment. As they straightened up they hesitated, eyes shut, briefly savouring the moment of their return, breathing in the sharp, misty night air of their home. A brief flurry of heavy raindrops fell, spotting their dusty black cloaks. Above them great masses of grey cloud blew slowly over the mountain, obscuring the tops of the highest towers, their grey shapes blending with the darkness of the night sky.

To one side of the spur was a deep cleft and within it was a staircase – carved into the split in the rock and following its meandering path to the ground. Down this Muesli and Corpus sped – both of them hoping against hope they would meet no one who was on the way up. Their luck held and, moments later, they emerged from the stairway into a narrow lane that zigzagged down between windowless castle walls to a glistening ribbon of cobbled roadway below. Once on the rain-slick cobbles the pair turned left and, keeping to the deepest shadows, hurried past dark doorways and shuttered windows until, running through an archway, they arrived in an enclosed yard.

Muesli suddenly gripped Corpus's arm and pulled him back into the shadows. From a passage on the far side of the yard three vampires emerged, dragging another along the ground on the end of a length of rope. The trussed vampire struggled to get up but each time he was roughly knocked to the ground again.

Muesli felt Corpus bristle with rage beside him. He shook his head vehemently and mouthed the word 'Wait' to his angry friend.

The struggling figure was hauled across the flagstones and into another passage, the raucous laughter of his captors echoing in the confined space.

Quickly the two friends leapt out of hiding and raced across the yard. Reaching the passage they carefully spied round the corner at the retreating figures. Another vampire appeared at the far end and waved at the approaching group.

Muesli and Corpus quickly pulled back out of sight.

'Nothing we can do now, Corpy,' whispered Muesli grimly. 'The jail is at the end of that passage, in the next square. That's where they're going.'

Corpus let out a long, pent-up breath of frustration.

'I could have taken them, Mooz,' he whispered fiercely. 'That was old Vennel they were manhandling. He never did anyone any harm.'

Muesli nodded grimly.

'I know, Corpy,' he said quietly, 'but we couldn't risk doing anything that would bring attention to us. Especially out in the open here. What if one of them had escaped? The cat would have been out of the bag then, wouldn't it? Fibula would have found out we were back.' He sighed. 'Vennel will be safe enough in jail until we can free him . . . and everyone else.'

'You're right, of course,' replied Corpus, his big shoulders relaxing. 'But it just made my blood boil to see those three cowards roughing up old Ven like that.'

Keeping close to the walls they crossed to the other side of the yard, passed through an archway and ran lightly down a winding, cobbled lane.

Halfway down the slope they came across the wreckage of a coffincar – its wheels buckled and mahogany sides caved in. It leant sadly against the wall like a huge, damaged insect.

'It's Vennel's, Corpy,' Muesli whispered, anger in his eyes. 'I helped him build it.' He shook his head. 'As if taking him to prison wasn't enough, they had to destroy this too!'

Coffincars had been invented by Muesli and now a number of vampires moved around Eyetooth in these mobile resting places instead of their traditional black hearses. Fibula hated them – they reminded him of Muesli.

There was a sudden scraping sound from above them as someone began to open a window.

Muesli and Corpus melted into the darkness beneath the overhanging lintels and sped lightly away, flitting along the lane like shadows. They were nearing the heart of Eyetooth.

Hurrying through a rock-cut passageway, they ran silently along a dripping arcade that curved down to a cobbled square.

Apart from a single torch that guttered above one of the doorways, the square was in darkness.

Muesli and Corpus gazed intently across the ancient paving to a tall, thin town house. Two narrow alleys, more like clefts in a rock face than passageways, separated the town house from the ugly castellated mansions that crowded in on either side.

'Alchema's place,' whispered Corpus, and Muesli nodded.

Skirting the side of the square furthest from the torchlight they moved silently and purposefully towards what they hoped would be the hiding place of their old friend.

Chapter Twenty-four

Count Fibula stood by the great front door of his castle, surrounded by his six chosen vampires.

'The mist will descend again soon . . . as always,' he mused. 'Something you can rely on in Eyetooth.' He turned to stare into Spitz's eyes. 'I trust your information will be as reliable.'

The large, bald-headed vampire did not flinch.

'I am confident that we will capture the ringleaders tomorrow night, Count Fibula,' he said smoothly.

Beside him stood Horba, whose eyes glittered as he smoothed his bushy moustache with a taloned forefinger.

'I too, Count, am certain,' his harsh voice rang out. 'They will not escape us this time. I am told that the conspirators will number a mere seven. Our forces number well over thirty.'

Fibula nodded in agreement.

'The odds are strongly in our favour. I approve.' He glanced at his other followers, then back at Spitz and Horba. 'Very well. After you root out the last traces of opposition from the tunnels tomorrow you will parade your captives in the prison square. I will issue a command that everyone must attend. Once they see Countess Alchema and her friends in chains they will realize that any further resistance is useless.' He smirked. 'I have waited a long time for this . . . I am going to enjoy it.'

The door set into the courtyard gates was suddenly thrown open with a crash, and all seven vampires spun round and stared, instinctively tensing for action.

A squat figure stumbled through the opening and scurried frantically towards them.

'Ichor!' hissed Fibula as his servant staggered up the steps and stood, panting heavily, trying to recover his breath. 'Why has it taken you so long? I asked you to find out the location of the Rattery and return immediately. Well?'

'Master . . .' gasped the bedraggled figure of Ichor, 'Master . . .'

'Out with it!'

'A-a vampire hunter has come!' Ichor blurted out, his wild eyes flitting from Fibula to the other vampires. 'I saw him in the tunnels. *He fired a silver pistol at me!*'

Fibula's eyes widened in disbelief and the others looked at each other uncertainly, unsure whether they had heard correctly.

'A *what*?' Fibula spat out, reaching forward and grasping hold of his servant's collar, pulling him close. 'A vampire hunter, you say?'

Ichor blanched at the nearness of the council leader's contorted, cruel face and nodded rapidly, trembling as he did so. 'Y-yes. "*I am a vampire hunter*," he cried. Then the vampire hunter pointed his gun at Vane . . .'

The brutal grip on Ichor's collar tightened suddenly, making the servant wince in pain.

'At *Vane*?' snapped Fibula. 'But you said he shot at *you*.' He thrust his thin, white face closer to Ichor's and croaked, 'Didn't you?'

107

Ichor's head jerked back under the force of his master's icy glare.

'Y-yes, Master,' replied Ichor, trembling even more. 'He-he did. The vampire hunter aimed at Vane but saw me moving beyond the light and fired at me instead.'

'And then?'

'I ran, Master. To tell you!'

Fibula abruptly released his grip and Ichor staggered backwards into Crusst. The hooded vampire pushed the servant disdainfully aside, causing Ichor to drop to his knees, gasping and massaging his neck.

'So,' hissed Fibula, 'you do not know if Vane was killed or if he escaped? Did you hear another shot?'

'No, Master,' whispered Ichor.

'Count Fibula,' Spitz interjected, 'there is a patrol in the tunnels at this moment. If they heard the shot, then –'

Fibula raised his hand for silence, and his eyes glittered.

'Yes,' he said. 'Indeed. If they were nearby then they may have attacked and captured the vampire hunter.'

'Or the vampire hunter may have killed *them*,' muttered Blech nervously.

Giving Blech a withering look, Fibula

spun on his heel and strode back into his castle.

The others followed, scurrying after their master and gathering round him in front of the great fireplace.

'A vampire hunter,' muttered Sleed half to himself, glancing sideways at his companions with a fearful expression on his gaunt, pale face. 'How did he find us?'

Looking for guidance, the vampires turned to their leader, who was regarding them from under furrowed brows.

'He must have obtained information from someone,' Fibula hissed softly. 'But from whom?' The leader of the council stared into the darkness beyond the candlelight and gradually the group saw his mouth slowly twist in a malevolent smile. 'It could be,' he went on, 'yes, just possible that he came upon our two *friends* – Muesli and Corpus – in the outside world and, before dispatching them, extracted the location of our refuge.'

There was a sharp intake of breath from the vampires.

'Yes. That could be the answer,' cried Scabrus. 'And if it is true then the hunter has done us all a favour.'

Spitz cracked his knuckles and glowered darkly.

'If it is true then it is a pity,' he growled. 'I had unfinished business with those two.'

'There is another alternative,' offered Crusst nervously, his thin fingers plucking at the edges of his mildewed cloak. 'The humans may have sent the vampire hunter here for revenge, perhaps even with the connivance of Muesli and Corpus. The traitors may still be alive . . . waiting outside the mountain for news.'

'But would vampires – even traitors like them – send a vampire hunter into Eye-tooth?' asked Blech tremulously, his pale eyes flicking from one face to the next.

'Why not?' rasped Fibula. Agitatedly he fingered the golden amulet at the neck of his high-collared shirt and then spun away from them, his cloak swinging out, making smoke gust out from the fireplace. He began to pace up and down, his bony hands clasped behind his back. 'Whether Muesli and Corpus are alive or dead is of no importance at the moment. The priority is the vampire hunter. He must be found!' He pointed at Spitz. 'How many tunnel entrances are there?'

Spitz frowned.

'Too many for us to cover, Count Fibula,' he replied.

Fibula scowled then suddenly cried, 'Ichor!'

The squat servant scurried to Count Fibula's side.

'Which exit did you use from the tunnels?' Fibula demanded.

'The one under the Howling Bridge, Master,' answered Ichor quickly.

'Very well,' said Fibula, turning to Spitz and Horba, 'you will concentrate a force there. If Ichor came out of that hole then it is quite possible that our quarry will do the same.' He paused for a moment then asked, 'When is the tunnel patrol due to report back?'

'In thirty minutes, Count Fibula,' responded Horba.

'Then that's when we will know where we stand,' said Fibula. 'When we will know whether the vampire hunter has been captured or not.'

There was a short, awkward silence, broken eventually by Crusst.

'Vampire hunters are meant to be difficult to overcome, Count Fibula,' he muttered nervously. 'It is said that they alone among humans are immune to the hypnotic powers of *the voice*. If that is so, how would he be defeated . . .?'

'I am your leader!' Fibula roared suddenly, flinging his arms wide and fixing them all with a withering, furious stare. 'While you are under my command you will fear no one. Do you hear? No one! *Not even a vampire hunter!*'

He strode past them to the centre of the room, then spun round, his black cloak swinging out behind him, a living part of the surrounding shadows.

'This is a priority,' he hissed. 'All my followers are to be redirected to this task. Those not at the Howling Bridge will search Eyetooth. The vampire hunter *will* be found! Go now and brief your underlings to the task ahead.' His red eyes seemed to catch fire in the candlelight. '*Nothing will stand in my way.*'

Chapter Twenty-five

Joe, Vinny and Anthonia stumbled along the winding tunnel, pulled by the ropes that bound their wrists. Their captors sometimes jerked roughly on the ropes, sniggering when it drew gasps of pain from their victims.

Each of the three prisoners was led by a vampire while the fourth vampire strode ahead, holding up a lantern to guide their way through the tunnel maze.

The attack had taken Joe and the others completely by surprise and they had been overwhelmed easily. Vinny, ferociously pushed into a pillar, had bumped his head and, dazed, had taken no further part in the fight. Vane had attempted to hit one of the assailants with his umbrella but had been thrown aside scornfully, while Joe and Anthonia had struggled but were no match for the four vampires.

As their attackers bound their hands it was discovered that Vane had disappeared.

Anthonia had been furiously contemptuous.

'He's your friend?' she had whispered fiercely in Joe's ear. 'So why did he run? To save his own miserable skin, that's why. None of his kind can be trusted. They are pitiful creatures!'

Joe knew that this wasn't true but couldn't face arguing with Anthonia, as he was too concerned about his father. Vinny had a gash on the side of his temple and was stumbling along groggily.

At that moment the vampire leading Vinny turned, his cruel face outlined in the lamplight. 'Keep moving!' he snarled, jerking the rope hard and making Vinny grimace.

'You OK, Dad?' Joe asked anxiously as the vampire turned away again.

Vinny smiled tightly.

'I'm fine, Joe,' he murmured. 'Don't worry, I'll think of something.'

Joe smiled back but a cold, nagging fear had begun to work its way upwards from his stomach. He didn't hold out much hope of them being rescued in the tunnels – and once in Eyetooth their fate would be sealed. He tried to think positively, if only to calm his fears. To his left Anthonia was staring straight ahead, her eyes burning, her mouth set in a grim line. Another thing that chilled Joe was the fact that he could see the vampires continually stealing covert glances over their shoulders, once or twice deliberately licking their lips. The only thing stopping them from biting us right here and now, thought Joe, was their fear of Fibula. He had overheard them hoarsely whisper to each other that 'the master' would be pleased with their capture of the three outsiders . . . and might *reward them with some human blood*.

As if he had read Joe's thoughts, his captor leant towards his companion and hissed, 'Blood! I feel the need for it now that I am so close to . . .' he jerked his hooded head backwards, 'such a large supply!'

His companion cackled and turned his thin, bearded face round to stare malevolently at Joe.

115

'I too am thirsty,' he muttered harshly. 'Just the smallest taste would satisfy.'

'We cannot,' replied his friend regretfully. 'The master . . .'

'I know,' snapped the bearded one peevishly. 'I know!'

The leading vampire halted abruptly and swept his lantern in an arc over the ground at his feet as a black shape fled from the pool of light.

'Did you see that?' he demanded hoarsely of his companions. 'A rat! A nice fat one!'

The other vampires hurried forward, searching eagerly around them.

'But how can this be?' muttered the hooded vampire, jerking Joe after him as he moved forward. 'There are no rats in the tunnels.'

'Except,' the light-bearer said slowly, '*in the Rattery*!' He lifted his lantern to the side and pointed to a narrow opening in the tunnel wall. 'The rat came from in there.' He thrust the lantern through the opening. 'It's another tunnel.'

The bearded vampire cackled again.

'We may have just discovered the location of the secret breeding place. Just think,' he gloated, 'of all those fat rats in there, all that succulent flesh and blood – just waiting to be enjoyed!'

The other vampires licked their lips.

'Yes,' murmured the vampire who had not yet spoken – a thin, wizened figure with straggling, dirty fair hair. 'Just waiting . . . *for us!*'

'My thirst needs to be slaked – *now*,' said the lantern-bearer greedily. 'I'm sure a small detour would take us no time at all. Agreed?'

'Agreed!' chorused the other three.

The light-bearer stepped through the narrow opening and one by one the other vampires followed in single file, each dragging a captive behind them.

The tunnel was roughly hewn and seemed almost as narrow as an arrow slit. It turned and twisted and from time to time Joe could see dark, deep openings on either side of the path. From these deep clefts wafted an unpleasant, pungent smell.

'Rats!' hissed the vampires, gulping in the odour greedily as they passed. After only a minute or so the tunnel widened out into a high chamber, pitted all around with deep niches set high up in the walls. It appeared to be a dead end.

Last to be hauled into this chamber, Joe only had time to register his surroundings before several black shapes suddenly dropped from the niches with a soft flurrying sound like the beating of large wings.

The light went out and the pitch-black chamber became a cauldron of hissing, scuffling and threshing as the four vampires tried to fight off their attackers.

Knocked to the ground, Joe frantically attempted to scramble away from the writhing bodies around him. Someone grabbed him by the arm but he lashed out, using his bound hands like a club, striking a shoulder.

'Get off!' he shouted amid the screeching and howling of the vampires.

'Ow! Joe! It's me!' gasped Vinny in his ear. 'Are you OK?'

'Dad!' Joe cried, grasping his father's elbow. 'Yeah . . . I'm fine.'

'Where's Anthonia?' Vinny exclaimed hoarsely. 'She still here?'

Just then a voice hissed at them sharply above all the noise and they felt the ropes round their wrists being tugged.

'*Come with me.*'

'Vane!' cried Joe in delight. 'It's you.'

'Come now,' insisted the little werewolf, giving the ropes another tug.

'What about Anthonia?' cried Joe.

'I have her,' replied Vane tersely. 'She's hurt her ankle.'

Allowing themselves to be led through the darkness by the pull of the ropes, they escaped from the fray. When they realized they were once more in the tunnel they stood up and hurried as fast as Anthonia's limping gait would permit.

Vane led them into one of the narrow side openings. This broadened out after a few twists and turns and Vane stopped and lit his lantern. They were in a low tunnel with silence round them as thick as fog, the sounds of the struggle behind them having been swallowed up by the mountain. As the light flared Joe caught Anthonia's expression as she stared at the little werewolf. Her look was still cold but Joe was sure he detected a faint note of uncertainty in it too.

Laying the lantern on the ground, Vane hooked his umbrella over one arm, took out a knife from an inside pocket and quickly cut the ropes.

Joe and Vinny immediately began to massage their sore wrists. Anthonia did this briefly too but then, kneeling, started to rub her right ankle.

'How is it?' asked Vinny.

'I'll live,' responded Anthonia sharply.

Vinny shrugged but Joe frowned.

'Now do you see, Anthonia?' he said quietly. 'Vane didn't run away to save his own skin. He did it to save us.'

Anthonia didn't reply but her ankle-rubbing suddenly became fiercer.

Vinny patted the little werewolf on the shoulder.

'Thanks, Vane,' he said. 'I take it the rat in the tunnel was sent out deliberately to entice the vampires in? But,' his brows furrowed, 'how did you know they would fall for it?'

Vane smiled, the points of his sharp little teeth showing briefly against his leathery and whiskery lips.

'They're greedy,' he said simply. 'And the Rattery guards were pleased to help me. They hate Fibula.' He became serious again. 'We must go now,' he went on. 'The longer you remain in the tunnels the greater the danger. I must return to Eyetooth but I will guide you out of the mountain first. Not far from here the way branches. Left takes you down; right, up.' He blinked. 'We will go left,' he said.

Joe stole a glance at Anthonia as Vane said this but the girl's face betrayed no hint of emotion.

'Just be careful as you follow me,' said Vane. 'Keep to the centre of the path. There are loose rocks and holes on either side. The tunnel forks not far ahead.'

Vane lifted his lantern as high as he could and set off again along the tunnel.

Vinny gestured for Joe to go first and for Anthonia to follow.

The girl shot him a look of annoyance before hobbling after Joe and Vane.

Vinny brought up the rear, shining his torch on the pathway to make it easier for them all to avoid the loose rocks and dark openings that Vane had warned them about.

After a hundred metres or so Vane glanced over his shoulder. 'Nearly at the fork,' he said.

Vinny looked up, momentarily taking his eyes off the ground in front of him. Suddenly his left leg slid on the loose stones and shot into a hole. Unable to stop himself falling, he felt his right knee strike the ground at the edge of the hole and, with a soft rushing sound, the edge gave way. Stones and small debris toppled into the widening gap with a tumbling rush – and so did Vinny, still clutching on to his torch.

'Hey!' he yelled in fright as he plunged downwards out of sight.

Horrified, Joe leapt forward.

'Dad!' he shouted in panic, dropping to his knees by the edge of the hole. 'Dad!'

Vane and Anthonia joined him as faint surprised shouts of, 'Hey! Whoa! Ow!' came drifting out of the hole, gradually fading out as the mountain rock swallowed them.

Vane grasped a frantic Joe by the arm.

'Do not worry, Joe,' he said quickly. 'This area is like a honeycomb. Holes like this one are actually small tunnels that connect to larger ones. Your father will most probably slide into one of those. I will go after him. You two go on to the tunnel fork and remain there.' The little werewolf abruptly sat down and swung his short legs into the hole. He looked into Joe's face intently. 'I will bring your father back via the left tunnel . . . but it may take me a little while.'

Joe gulped and nodded, his face betraying his anxiety.

'We'll wait for you.'

'Do you have a torch?'

'I have a small one in my bag,' Anthonia replied, sliding her rucksack from her shoulders and delving into a side pocket.

'Very well,' Vane said as Anthonia switched on the torch and shone it into the hole.

With some relief Joe could see that the hole, far from plunging straight down as he had feared, actually sloped away at a steep angle.

'I'll go now,' Vane went on, grasping his umbrella close to his body and holding the lantern above his head.

'Good luck,' Joe said fervently.

'Thank you,' replied the little werewolf, and, with that, he slipped over the edge and was gone.

Chapter Twenty-six

Vinny slid down out of the hole and bumped, unharmed but shaken, on to a hard, flat surface, followed by a shower of small stones and gritty dust. He sat blinking and sneezing before pulling out a hankie, wiping his eyes and face and blowing his nose. During the terrifying downward rush he had remembered thinking a ridiculous thought – *I wish I had my movie camera with me . . . this would make an excellent shot!*

'You're mad, Vinny,' he muttered. 'Imagine thinking a thing like that when you could have been sliding into goodness knows where!'

Scrambling into a kneeling position he picked up the torch and shone it into the hole he had just fallen out of. It was immediately obvious that it would be impossible to climb back up. The slope was too steep, its sides too smooth and the space too tight.

'Hello!' he shouted. 'Can you hear me? Joe? Vane?'

There was no reply. Sighing, he shone the torch around himself and found he was in another tunnel.

'Now what?' he muttered. A faint sound startled him and he backed up against the rocky wall, flashing his torch left and right, trying unsuccessfully to make out where the sound was coming from. After a moment he realized it was coming from the hole – a dull rattling, rushing sound that was quickly getting louder. Suddenly a small, black shape shot out of the hole accompanied by a scatter of pebbles. Skidding across the ground it came to rest at his feet.

The small figure shook itself and a hairy face looked up at Vinny.

Vinny gasped in delight.

'Vane!' he cried. 'Am I glad to see you!'

The little werewolf got to his feet and

lifted his lantern up so that it illuminated Vinny's face.

'Are you hurt?' he asked.

'I'm fine.' replied Vinny. 'Hunky-dory. Just hope Joe's not too worried about me.' He grinned with relief and pointed upwards. 'I hope you've come to lead me back?'

'I have indeed,' replied Vane.

'Great. Let's go. Which way?'

Vane looked left and right and frowned.

'It may not be as easy as you think,' he said thoughtfully. 'As you will have realized, we can't go back up the way we came down.' He tapped the tip of his umbrella agitatedly on the stony ground as he looked around. 'I have a map of these tunnels in my head but I do not recognize this place. I do not believe I have passed this way before.' The wrinkles on his hairy brows deepened. 'Which way?' he muttered to himself. 'Right or left?' After a moment's consideration he lifted his brolly and pointed left. 'This way,' he said.

'Lead on,' replied Vinny as brightly as he could.

The tunnel snaked off into the mountain, always curving left. After fifteen minutes

Vane suddenly halted and Vinny almost walked into him.

'What's up?' asked Vinny, wiping his brow. He switched on his torch and played it ahead of them. 'Ah,' he said, as he saw that the tunnel had come to a dead end. 'I see.'

Without a word Vane turned round and began to trot quickly back the way they had come.

Vinny took a deep breath, sighed and followed him.

They passed the spot from which they had started and kept going. The pathway in this direction was almost a mirror image of the one they had just taken – continually curving right. As they hurried along Vinny began to have the queasy feeling that it would also end in the same way.

Fifteen minutes later it did precisely that.

'It was Vane's turn to say, 'Ah!' The werewolf held up his lantern, scouring the featureless rock of the dead end for another opening but there was none.

'I have heard of places like these,' he murmured, shaking his head worriedly, 'but never encountered one until now.'

'Places like what?' Vinny asked.

'Horseshoes,' replied Vane. 'Curved tunnels with no exits.'

Vinny stared at him, their predicament slowly dawning on him.

'What? You mean . . . we're trapped?'

Vane looked up at Vinny, his moist brown eyes glistening in the lantern's light.

'It would seem so,' he replied.

Chapter Twenty-seven

Anthonia sat on the ground by the fork in the tunnel, alternately rubbing and gently rotating her ankle. The torch was propped on top of her folded leather jacket and directed at her raised foot.

Joe sat opposite her, his back against the rocky wall, scuffing his trainers over the dusty rock floor.

'Why did you fire the gun?' he asked quietly. 'I saw you jerk just before you did it. Did you miss Vane on purpose?'

'No!' the reply was scornful.

'What, then?'

Anthonia didn't reply for almost a minute as she concentrated on her ankle.

'I was distracted,' she said at last.

'By what?'

'Someone among the pillars. Could've been one of those vampires, I don't know. My hand jumped and the gun went off. It was an accident.'

Joe glared at her.

'So you really meant to shoot Vane?'

'Of course. And I would have after that if you hadn't grabbed me.'

Joe frowned angrily.

'But you saw how good he is! He saved us from the vampires!'

'Maybe,' said Anthonia.

'No maybes about it,' Joe replied hotly. 'Definitely! Anyway,' he went on, 'how could you do something like that? Point a gun at someone, I mean.'

'It was my great-grandmother's gun,' Anthonia replied fiercely. 'Passed on to me. I am following in her footsteps. Doing what she did.'

'You mean . . . she *killed* vampires with it?'

'Yes.'

'Well, I'm glad it's gone!' Joe said forcefully. 'I hate guns!'

Anthonia shrugged and, leaning forward,

picked up a small stone. She examined it quietly in the torchlight, then placed it in her jacket pocket and went back to massaging her foot.

There was another long silence – Joe's thoughts drifting anxiously to his father.

'How is your ankle?' he asked eventually.

'Better,' answered Anthonia. 'Much better.'

'That's good.'

The girl gave her ankle one more slow turn, picked up the torch and carefully got to her feet.

'It is,' she replied, cautiously trying her weight on her right foot. Satisfied, she looked up. 'Means I can go on.'

'What?' Joe was startled. He stood up quickly and stared at Anthonia as she picked up her jacket and put it on. 'What do you mean?'

Anthonia pointed at the right-hand tunnel.

'On,' she repeated. 'Up to Eyetooth. I have a job to do.'

'You can't mean it. I . . . I thought you'd decided not to. I mean . . . you're no match for a vampire. And now that you haven't got your stupid little gun with you, you'll get caught easily. You saw how simple it was for those vampires to capture us.'

'I was taken by surprise. It won't happen again. I know what to expect now.'

'No, you don't,' exclaimed Joe furiously. 'You don't know the half of it. There's a battle going on up there between good vampires and bad vampires. Good vampires just want to be left in peace. They only drink rats' blood . . . they don't harm humans.'

'I don't believe there is such a thing as a good vampire,' returned Anthonia, scowling. 'From what I've seen so far they're all bad – exactly like my great-grandmother said in her diary.'

Joe groaned in frustration. I just can't get through to her, he thought. But I've got to try.

'You can't go on. You just can't. I won't let you!'

Anthonia's eyes narrowed. A head taller than Joe she looked down at him scornfully.

'You're a brave boy, Joe, but you're not big enough or strong enough to stop me.'

'So how do you expect to . . . to *remove* the vampires, then?' Joe tried to sound as scornful as her. '*Talk* them to death?'

'I have my ways,' she answered.

'Like what?' Joe asked, then frowned suspiciously as a thought struck him. 'Hey! What's in your rucksack? Not another gun?'

'No,' Anthonia retorted. 'And anyway, what's in there is my business.'

'But . . .' Joe began desperately.

'Save it,' retorted Anthonia sharply. 'I'm going.'

Turning away from him, Anthonia walked purposefully, but still with a slight limp, towards the right-hand tunnel entrance.

Joe was confused. What should he do? He couldn't just watch as she walked away to a horrible fate. Why couldn't he go with her – try and change her mind? Look out for her? But what would Vane and his dad think when they came back? He couldn't let them believe he had been taken. But then another thought struck him. Anthonia had said that she had been distracted by some-one among the pillars – one of the vampires that had attacked them . . . but what if it wasn't? What if it was someone else who had then run off to tell Fibula? If that was the case, then Fibula would now know about the return of Muesli and Corpus. Joe's two vampire friends would be in great danger!

133

That decided him. He would follow Anthonia and hope that Vane would find out what he had done somehow, take Vinny to a safe place and then come after them.

'Wait!' he called as Anthonia entered the tunnel.

She stopped and turned, her torch still directed along the passageway.

'What?'

'I'm coming with you.'

Anthonia looked startled.

'No, you're not.'

'I am . . . and you can't stop me.'

She glared at him.

'Don't think you can prevent me from fulfilling my destiny, Joe,' she said coldly. 'You can't, so coming with me is point-less.'

Joe glared back.

'We'll see about that,' he said.

Anthonia's eyes narrowed then she shrugged. 'It's your funeral,' she replied and, turning her back, continued on her way.

I hope I'm doing the right thing, Joe thought. Taking a deep breath he quickly followed Anthonia through the opening. Dogging her footsteps, he watched the circle of torchlight move steadily ahead of her on the rocky floor of the tunnel as it turned and twisted its way upwards through the darkness, taking them ever nearer to Eyetooth.

Chapter Twenty-eight

Muesli and Corpus moved silently up the high side wall of Alchema's house, their black-cloaked shapes lost in the darkness of the alley.

'Here,' hissed Muesli as he found the deep recess near the top. 'Alchema once told me she always kept this window open.' Carefully he climbed into the room beyond and Corpus followed, grunting as he squeezed his broad shoulders through the gap.

The two vampires' keen night vision enabled them to see every detail of the book-lined room. They were in Alchema's study.

At the door, Muesli listened for signs of life. The house was silent. Beyond the door was a landing protected by an ornate wooden banister.

Muesli leapt lightly on to the banister rail. Balancing like a tightrope walker above the deep and dark stairwell, he stretched up and tapped out a short staccato code on the carved mahogany ceiling.

From above came a faint scraping sound and a moment later one of the oak panels was lifted upwards and a pale face appeared in the gap, a mass of silver hair glinting faintly in the gloom.

'Countess Alchema!' whispered Muesli with delight. 'We've come back!'

'Muesli!' cried Alchema joyfully. 'And Corpus! Oh . . . it's so good to see you both again. Come up!'

Her head disappeared, there was a faint rattling sound and a ladder slid downwards from the hatchway. Moments later both Muesli and Corpus were in Alchema's secret room, the ladder stowed and the hatch safely shut again. A shuttered lantern cast a muted yellow glow around the cramped attic space, diffusing the edges of a small bookcase, a table and a chair and throwing shadows over Alchema's bed of earth under the eaves.

'How have you been, Countess?' asked Muesli with concern after they had greeted each other properly. 'Have you fully recovered?'

The countess gave the young vampire a wan smile. 'My fight with Fibula left me very weak for some time, certainly,' she replied, 'but yes, I have recovered. I couldn't have done it without Bray, though. She was magnificent – brought me here, tended me and kept me informed of Fibula's activities.' Alchema gestured around her hiding place. 'I do well enough. Fibula's minions searched the house but didn't find me. They locked the windows and nailed the outside doors fast. But,' she smiled grimly, 'I can move around the house more or less at will and so am able to open windows to allow access to our friends.'

'We've heard that many of them are now in prison,' Corpus said morosely. He cracked his knuckles. 'I'm itching to go to the jail to free them.'

'That would be very difficult,' answered Alchema, 'as it is well guarded. But it is an option that we will be discussing at our meeting tomorrow. Yes,' she went on, smiling at the two vampires' raised eyebrows, 'your arrival is indeed timely. A meeting of the remaining *rebels*, as Fibula calls us, will take place tomorrow night. They will be greatly cheered to see you.' She looked into their eyes with a fierce intensity. 'It is do or die,' she said. 'If Fibula defeats us then I fear for Eyetooth. The mountain will not hold its secret once he sends his followers out into the world to attack humans again. For the last week or so I have watched Fibula's henchmen take over the streets, jailing anyone they do not like.'

'Watched?' Muesli looked puzzled. 'Do you mean you have been outside?'

Alchema smiled bleakly. 'Oh yes,' she replied quietly. 'I have become quite adept at travelling unseen throughout Eyetooth.'

Muesli leant forward, an intense look in his eyes.

'Then let's not wait for tomorrow,' he said forcefully. 'We met Vane as we came here and he informed us that Fibula plans to act in the next few days. He would have told you but was sent to the Rattery by Fibula. I believe we cannot afford to wait. We should find our friends and fight back tonight!'

139

Corpus's eyes lit up and he glanced eagerly at Alchema.

'Mooz is right, Countess,' he said. 'Let's do it now.' He grinned impishly. 'And if our route takes us past my house I'd like to pop in for a moment; there's a hidden bottle of vintage Fangola I'd like to liberate. We'll drink to our success.'

Alchema looked from one to the other, the severe planes of her noble face softening as a smile touched her lips.

'Your presence fills me with renewed vigour,' she said. 'You both have a way of making me feel young again. 'And you, Muesli . . . I'd almost forgotten just what a man of action you have become. So, indeed, let us go.'

Chapter Twenty-nine

'What did you do that for?' Joe asked as Anthonia switched off her torch, plunging them into complete darkness. Reaching forward blindly he encountered her rucksack, his hand closing on one of the straps. He gave it a jerk. 'Trying to get away from me in the dark?'

'Shh! I can feel a breath of cool air on my face,' she hissed. 'We must be near a way out.'

Joe realized he could feel the air too. It felt good after having breathed the heavy tunnel air for so long. Anthonia began to move forward again with Joe keeping a firm grip on the strap with his right hand while stretching out with the fingers of his left to brush the tunnel wall. Joe noticed that the tunnel walls were now damp to the touch. The path began to rise steeply and after a few minutes he could see a narrow opening ahead, blue-grey against the surrounding black. The air around them felt cold now and he shivered slightly, letting go of the rucksack so that he could zip up his padded jacket.

He saw Anthonia's shape silhouetted against the opening as she hurried ahead.

'Careful!' he whispered hoarsely.

She slowed down and Joe caught up with her. Together they moved silently up the final ramp.

As they cautiously emerged into the open Joe looked around anxiously, tensed and ready to run at the first sign of trouble.

Although it was not actually raining, the air was saturated with moisture and felt wet against Joe's face.

He and Anthonia found they were on a ledge that jutted from the side of a sheer face of rock. Facing them across a broad gap was a castle wall beyond which towers and turrets loomed darkly through the gloom. Anthonia seemed transfixed by this sight.

'At last . . . Eyetooth,' she breathed.

Not far below them was a narrow gully that disappeared behind a rocky outcrop on their left. Joe looked the other way and immediately froze. Not far off, almost indistinguishable from the shadows of the buildings on either side, were seven or eight vampires. They were gathered by a thin, arching bridge and so far the vampires hadn't seen them. Joe reached out to warn Anthonia but realized she had moved away and was running lightly down a pathway cut into the rock face, her ankle obviously no longer troubling her.

The vampires will see her, he thought. Hurrying in pursuit, he reached her a few steps from the bottom.

'Vampires!' he whispered urgently, pointing, as she looked back at him. 'Over there.'

Anthonia spun round. She stared hard into the darkness between the overhanging buildings then smiled in delight.

'I see them.'

'Let's go back up,' hissed Joe anxiously. 'Before they see us. Come on!'

Instead of following him, Anthonia swung the rucksack off her shoulders and squatted down on the bottom steps, undoing the straps.

'What are you doing?'

Anthonia glared at him.

'Back off,' she muttered savagely. 'This is what I came here to do.'

'No way,' gasped Joe. Lunging forward he grabbed for the rucksack but only managed to get a grip on one of the flaps.

Furious, Anthonia jerked it out of his grasp so violently that the rucksack swung back sharply and struck the rock face beside her, sending a cascade of small stones rattling downwards on to the bed of the gully.

Joe looked towards the vampires and groaned in despair. All seven vampires were staring in their direction. As he watched, four of the vampires detached themselves from the group and began racing towards them, cloaks flying. Frantically he grasped Anthonia by the arm.

'They're coming,' he croaked in panic 'Come on!'

Anthonia tried to shake him off, intent on pulling something out of her bag.

'Come *on*!' yelped Joe. He yanked at the rucksack again. 'Now!'

'Nnrrgh!' Anthonia let out a stifled scream of exasperation. Glancing up she saw the vampires were now only fifty metres away and approaching fast. Thrusting the rucksack under her arm she leapt down the last few steps and, followed by Joe, sprinted away along the gully.

Rounding the corner they clambered breathlessly up the side of the gully into a lane that ran between two dark buildings.

Once in the lane Anthonia flew ahead, the gap between them increasing swiftly as they raced on. Joe struggled to keep up with the pace of the long-legged girl.

Anthonia glanced over her shoulder.

'Faster!' she yelled.

Joe heard a hoarse cry behind him and knew that the vampires were in the lane now too. Up ahead he saw Anthonia suddenly dart to the right and disappear into a dark passageway.

A surge of adrenalin ran through him and, putting on a spurt, he reached the passage a moment later and dived through it into an inner courtyard. He was just in time to see Anthonia climb through the open window of one of the derelict houses there. Haring across the yard Joe quickly followed suit, clambering over the high sill and dropping into the rot-smelling darkness below. He heard the sound of footsteps above him and realized that Anthonia had continued on up to the first floor.

At that moment he also heard the sound of the vampires in the passageway. Joe shrank against the wall below the window, hardly daring to breathe. After a few seconds he realized that the vampires had not come into the yard but were talking together in the passageway, their whispers echoing strangely in the confined space.

Maybe I should make a dash for it now? he thought.

Taking a deep breath he slowly raised himself until he could peer out round the side of the broken window.

Their hasty discussion over, the vampires were beginning to emerge stealthily into the yard.

All of a sudden Joe heard a strange, short, *thunk* from upstairs and, a fraction of a second later, a howl of pain from one of the vampires. With a start Joe saw the leading vampire stagger backwards and clutch wildly at the thin stake embedded in his shoulder. Joe gawped in disbelief. *Anthonia*

had shot him with some sort of arrow.
That's what she had in her rucksack!

The three other vampires turned tail and vanished into the passageway like weasels down a rabbit hole, leaving their wounded companion to get out as best he could before another stake-dart found him. Joe could hear them clattering away up the lane, back the way they had come, followed by the stumbling footsteps and whining curses of the injured vampire.

'Joe?'

Joe stuck his head out of the window and looked up. Anthonia was looking down at him from the upstairs window.

'What?' asked Joe.

The girl touched the brim of her hat in a jaunty gesture of farewell.

'Go back and wait for your father. I'm going on. Alone.'

'No, you can't. Wait.' Panicked, Joe pounded up the stone staircase but found no trace of Anthonia in any of the dank, empty rooms.

Frantically he raced back down the staircase and out into the middle of the yard. He scanned the broken rooftops of the derelict buildings and knew the truth with a sinking heart. Anthonia had disappeared.

She had deserted him – intent only on fulfilling her mad destiny.

The full horror of it hit him hard.

He was alone in Eyetooth.

Chapter Thirty

Having reported their failure to a furious Spitz, the fleeing vampires were now trailing wretchedly away. Spitz watched them go, his lips twisting in disdain. 'They are a disgrace,' he hissed. 'They encountered the vampire hunter and they *ran away*. Fools! Cowards!'

Beside him, Horba nodded his head in agreement, his expression contemptuous.

'Four of them went in pursuit. *Four!*' The moustached vampire's face contorted in a sneer. 'Any *one* of us here could have taken him!' He glanced round his own group. 'Isn't that true?'

'It is,' said Scabrus and Crusst together.

'The pity is,' Spitz muttered harshly, 'that the wrong people were in the right place.' He frowned thoughtfully. 'I wonder who the vampire hunter's small companion was – some kind of apprentice to the hunter, perhaps.'

'I don't know, Spitz,' Crusst replied. 'But I do know that the vampire hunter is armed and dangerous.'

Spitz gave him a black look. 'Yes,' he hissed. 'And we also know that the vampire hunter has eluded us and is now in Eyetooth.' He turned away. 'So – our vigil here is no longer necessary.'

'What about the tunnel patrol?' ventured Scabrus. 'Have they returned?'

Spitz's stare was icy.

'No. But that does not mean that the vampire hunter took them.'

'What other explanation is there?' asked Scabrus.

'Explanation?' cried Spitz, suddenly furious. 'The only explanation you should be worried about is the one we will have to give to Count Fibula for failing to capture the vampire hunter.' He turned to the others. 'Our mission is plain. The vampire hunter must be taken – dead or alive!'

Chapter Thirty-one

Anthonia crouched on a wall in the shadows of a jutting balcony. A fine rain was beginning to fall. Clutched in her right hand was her small crossbow, its curved bow and oak shaft glistening with moisture. Below her a narrow alley snaked away downhill.

Making sure there was no one about, she sprang lightly to the ground and sped off along the cobbled pathway.

She felt annoyed with herself. A true vampire hunter like her great-grandmother would not have missed with her first shot, she thought. True, she had struck the vampire on the shoulder but that was not good enough. Only a direct hit to the heart would kill the undead. She would have to do better next time.

Eyetooth was certainly living up to her expectations. For years she had researched vampire lore, reading old stories and folk tales and, recently, gathering local legends about the existence of a secret vampire refuge – building up a picture in her mind of what it would be like. And now she was here. Her sense of her mission was overpowering – and having survived two encounters with her sworn enemies she was more determined than ever.

The lane ended at the bottom of a set of worn stone steps and Anthonia crept up them silently, alert to any sound or movement. At the top she found herself on a thin walkway that ran between ancient battlements, designed as a vantage point for archers. As she began to cross she heard the sound of running feet from below. Cautiously looking down through a weathered arrow slit, she saw a group of vampires hurrying along the alleyway at the base of the ramparts. Torches were thrust into doorways and dark openings as the searchers went past.

Anthonia fitted a shaft to her crossbow and took aim but just as she did so the vampires suddenly disappeared from her line of sight. She could still hear them though – the echoey sound of their feet was drifting up from below. Realizing there must be an archway that cut into the ramparts from the alleyway, Anthonia sped away again, running lightly across the battlements, searching for the way down and, she hoped, an encounter with the vampires.

If they're looking for me, she thought grimly, they won't be glad to find me.

Halfway along the ramparts was a small opening that led to a series of steps and landings. The steps took Anthonia into the dark heart of a warren of narrow, winding passageways, each leading off the other and opening briefly out into tiny squares and courtyards.

Anthonia could still hear the sounds of the vampires but could not tell where they were coming from. Once or twice she halted, biting her lip in frustration, listening intently, trying to pinpoint their whereabouts but with no luck. The sounds seemed to have grown fainter. The vampires were going further away and Anthonia was losing them. Just at that moment she saw something – a vague shape moving on the other side of the square. Anthonia stepped back quickly and silently into an alcove and brought up her crossbow, staring fixedly over its sights, willing the shape to move out into the open.

It moved forward slightly and now Anthonia could see a hooded figure. The figure looked swiftly left and right, then walked rapidly . . . *directly towards her*.

Anthonia's finger tightened on the crossbow's trigger as she aimed the dart at the approaching vampire's heart.

This time, she thought. *This time.*

When the figure was barely twenty metres away she fired.

For Anthonia the next few seconds seemed to happen in slow motion. She heard the *thunk* of the wooden dart being released, saw it hurtle towards its target, saw the vampire stop in its tracks, fling up a hand . . . and *catch the arrow a microsecond before it struck home.*

Anthonia gasped in disbelief and was slow to react as the vampire, dart still clutched in its hand, leapt forward and bore down on her. She turned to flee but too late – the back of her neck was seized by a steely hand and she was hurled into the deepest recess of the alcove. She struck the wall and, twisting round, flailed with her fists, trying to beat off her assailant. But the vampire was on her like a cobra, pinning her into the corner and pointing the dart at Anthonia's throat.

'Assassin!' hissed the vampire.

Her heart pounding, Anthonia glared upwards at the hidden face.

'Yes!' she gasped defiantly. 'I am!'

The vampire suddenly let go of Anthonia's neck and, reaching up, pulled off her hat.

'You're just a girl!' the vampire cried, amazed. '*And human!*'

Then it was Anthonia's turn to gasp as the vampire slipped off its hood and the girl saw a pale, broad face and a tumble of greenish curls.

'You're a woman!'

The vampire bared her fangs. 'And a vampire,' she said darkly, leaning forward again to stare fiercely into Anthonia's eyes. 'Allow me to introduce myself – I am Countess Bray. And might I be allowed to know the name of the person who tried to end my life?'

Anthonia tried to look away but was held by the gaze of the countess's piercing eyes. She found herself saying, 'Anthonia.'

The countess moved slightly closer, her eyes glittering brightly.

'Who sent you here, Anthonia?'

'No one,' replied Anthonia sullenly. 'It was my own decision.'

'Your own decision to come here and kill vampires?'

'Yes.'

'Which vampires?'

'All vampires.'

Bray looked thoughtfully at her, then said briskly, 'I have to say you've got grit, girl. I could end your life very easily, you know. But I don't want to do it. No time for such things these days.' She peered at Anthonia intently. 'One more question . . . did you come here alone?'

'Yes,' Anthonia replied quickly.

The countess shook her head and tutted. 'No time for lies either,' she scolded. 'Never liked them. It's easy to tell when someone lies . . . especially a human.' She suddenly stood upright and listened, her head turned to the side. 'A patrol's coming,' she murmured.

Anthonia listened too but could hear nothing.

Bray got up, then reached forward and gripped Antonia by the arms, lifting her to her feet as if she weighed nothing.

'We have to talk further,' she whispered, 'so you have a decision to make. Either come with me quietly or be thrown to the patrol –' She looked down to the crossbow at their feet – 'without your dangerous little toy. Which?'

'I'll come,' replied Antonia quietly.

'The correct decision, my dear,' hissed Bray. Reaching down she picked up the crossbow, then gripping Anthonia firmly by the arm, led her quickly out of the alcove and into one of the narrow, twisting lanes that wormed their way into the heart of Eyetooth.

Chapter Thirty-two

Lost and bedraggled, Joe had been fruit-
lessly looking for Muesli and Corpus for
over an hour – constantly worrying about
his dad and Vane. All the twisting alleys
and passages had seemed the same to him,
and for the first half-hour he had run from
shadow to shadow in a panic, expecting to
be caught by Fibula's vampires at any
moment. Finding a bit of a chocolate bar in
his pocket had made him feel better and,
munching it, he had begun to look around
him and try to remember places he had seen
on his last visit. But nothing seemed familiar
and with his spirits sinking again he had
roamed deeper into Eyetooth's centre, the

occasional cries of searching vampires chilling his blood. But now, at last, he seemed to have had a real bit of luck. Keeping close to the damp base of a tower, he edged through the misty rain towards the shelter of a columned arcade that looked familiar.

I think I recognize this place, he thought. When I was here before, Muesli and I ran from Fibula's castle and I'm sure we went through that arcade on the way to Corpus's house. If I'm right it should lead on to a small square with an ancient fountain in the middle.

His heart beating fast with excitement, Joe darted into the arcade and hurried along under the cover of its dripping arches. At the end, the arcade turned sharply right. If he was correct then the little square should be round that corner. Reaching the corner he stopped to catch his breath, flattening himself against the ancient brickwork and crossing his fingers. He could hardly bear to look.

Inching forward he peered round the corner. He blinked. Was that a fountain out there in the centre of that space?

Yes, it was! Through the rain he recognized the stone obelisk. Corpus's house was not far away now – across the square and down an alley. He closed his eyes and wished hard that the big vampire and Muesli would be there.

He looked across the empty square again, having to quell a sudden urge to break cover and make a run for the alley on the other side. Don't do anything stupid now, Joe, he told himself – not when you're so close to the place you might find your friends. The buildings round the square looked un-inhabited and abandoned, their mouldering doors locked and barred and their windows shuttered. Centuries of foul weather had stained and blotched their old stones and, as Joe made his way feverishly from doorway to doorway, he could smell the decay that wafted from them, cold and unpleasant.

He was glad to leave the square and, entering the alley, the smell of wet and rot faded away behind him. Turning a corner, he entered the lane behind Corpus's house and broke into a run.

His destination was only fifty metres away when he skidded to a stop. There was someone by Corpus's back door! For one delirious moment his heart leapt as he thought, It's Corpus! – then, the jolting shock as the large cloaked figure turned and he saw who it was. Spitz! The bald vampire blinked in surprise and, reaching into the depths of the doorway without looking round, pulled someone else into view. Joe's horror was complete. The other figure was Horba. Both vampires now stared at Joe with vicious delight and began to move forward slowly.

Joe willed himself to move backwards . . . one foot at a time . . . away from those terrible eyes, those terrible talons. His skin felt like ice and his brain seemed to turn to stone. Where could he run to? Back the way he had come? No, that was too open. His only chance was to get among the maze of narrow passageways and rock-cut tunnels nearby – only there would he have a chance of losing them. Out of the corner of his eye he noticed a small, dark, arched opening in the lane wall. Without stopping to think he leapt across the lane and through. He found himself in a dripping, sewer-like tunnel and, heart pounding, tore frantically through the shallow puddles towards the faint shape of an opening far away at the other end. Behind him he heard a screech of laughter and, just as he reached the exit, a mocking shout that rolled along the tunnel behind him like a pursuing banshee.

'No need to hurry, boy . . . it's a dead end! A *dead* end for you!' Another shriek of laughter echoed along the dismal hole as the two vampires began their slow, crouching, laughing progress towards Joe.

Joe ran on and thought he was in the open but then realized at once they were right. He was trapped – in a space no bigger than a small room. Towering walls rose all round him to a height of some ten metres and, across the top, blackly silhouetted against the sodden night-grey clouds, stretched a latticed iron grille. A corroded iron gate lay to the side of the tunnel mouth he had just come from. He had run straight into a trap, into a disused, open-air prison. He felt chilled, empty, terrified. There was nowhere to go.

A sharp, grating noise above made him look up and he gasped again in fright. There were more vampires there! Five of them, all hooded, their black shapes hazy in the rain. One was already climbing through an opening in the latticed grille.

Drained of hope, Joe backed away until

his shoulders were pressed against the wet stone wall. The hooded vampire descended swiftly, arms and legs splayed out like a giant spider. From the middle of the tunnel Joe could hear the laughter and the echoey, mocking cries of Spitz and Horba as they approached: 'We're coming, boy. Nice and easy. Are you enjoying this, eh? Enjoying your last minutes in the birdcage? *We are!*'

Joe felt himself start to tremble and he clenched his fists tightly.

The hooded vampire leapt to the ground and spun round.

Joe started fearfully but still managed to swing up his fists. I'll give one of them a black eye at least, he thought.

The vampire leapt towards him, sweeping off its hood.

'Quick, Joe,' he hissed.

Joe stared, hardly able to believe what he saw, weak with shock and relief.

'*Corpus!*'

The big vampire grinned and turning, swiftly knelt in front of Joe.

'On my back, lad! Quickly!'

Arms tightly round Corpus's neck, Joe felt himself being swept effortlessly off the ground. In two strides the big vampire was at the wall and, without breaking his pace, sped straight upwards. The ascent was so smooth – the big vampire pulling them both higher and higher without, it seemed, touching the wall – that Joe felt like he was flying, carried upwards like a blown leaf. A wave of pure relief flooded through him at his escape.

At the top Corpus slipped through the opening and dropped the hatch with its broken lock back in place, with Joe still clinging to his broad back.

Joe peered through the rain at the cloaked and hooded figures who waited for them. Two of them he did not know but, with a tired grin of delight, he recognized the other two as Muesli and Alchema.

Without a word all five vampires turned and leapt from the grille on to a narrow stone walkway – and as they fled, Joe heard the first hoarse cries from Spitz and Horba as they entered the 'birdcage' – howls of rage and bafflement at discovering that their young, trapped bird had, mysteriously and inexplicably, *flown*.

Chapter Thirty-three

Vinny and Vane were beginning to despair. None of the holes they had found in the tunnel wall had been big enough to climb up. It was starting to look like they would never get out.

Vinny's worries about Joe and Anthonia were almost at panic level. I hope they're all right, he thought. I hope Fibula's vampires don't find them again. He slumped forward dejectedly, hands on his knees.

Suddenly Vane said, 'Ah. What's this?' Straightening quickly, Vinny saw that Vane was shining his lantern into a wide crack halfway up the tunnel wall.

'Yes,' breathed Vane. 'Interesting. It

seems to be large enough to accommodate your size, Vinny, and also slopes upwards at an easy angle.'

'We have to go for it, Vane,' replied Vinny. 'No choice.'

Quickly, Vinny helped Vane scramble into the hole, then climbed in himself.

'A tight fit but I think you will manage,' Vane called over his shoulder.

'Phew, see what you mean,' Vinny grunted as he inched his way along behind the little werewolf.

Their progress was slow but steady.

Vinny's elbows became numb as he pushed and scrabbled his way upwards. At times he had to wriggle worm-like through parts of the passageway that narrowed alarmingly, while at others he found he had enough room to crawl on his hands and knees. Dust got up his nose and small, loose stones, dislodged by Vane's feet, occasionally peppered his face.

Vinny frequently had to ask Vane to stop so that he could catch his breath. His mouth became so dry and his throat so parched that he began to fantasize about finding an underground stream and having a long, cool, reviving drink. He lost track of time and began to feel as if he had been burrowing through the earth forever.

At last an abrupt cry from Vane cut into his thoughts.

'What?' Vinny croaked.

'It's an opening!' cried Vane. 'There's a big space on the other side of it. I can feel a draught of air.'

'Whoo-ee!' cried Vinny in delight. 'Whoo-flipping-ee! We're out!'

Vane crawled forward through the opening and Vinny followed him. The little werewolf held up his lantern and they saw they were in an arched, stone passageway.

'Oh, we're not in the tunnels any more,' said Vane, puzzled, as they got to their feet.

'So where are we?' asked Vinny, his voice cracking with dryness. 'And more to the point, how do we get back to the tunnels to meet Joe and Anthonia?'

'Well,' answered Vane, 'I think the first thing we do is to get out of here.' He pointed. 'The passage ascends this way.'

They set off, tired and dusty, with Vane scanning the walls with his lantern as they went, looking for clues as to their whereabouts. The arched passage gradually became steeper and after a few hundred metres opened out into a large space. Vinny switched on his torch and played the beam around the walls. They were in a vaulted room with two, thick central pillars. The room was empty apart from two old barrels in one corner.

Vinny stared eagerly and licked his cracked lips.

'Those wouldn't be wine barrels, by any chance?' he said hopefully.

Vane padded over to them and peered at the faded printing on the side.

'No,' he replied as Vinny approached. 'They're full of Fangola.'

'The herbal vampire drink?' said Vinny. He reached past Vane and tried to lift the lid. 'I don't care what it is . . . I'll drink it!'

'Not without my permission, you won't!'

Vinny jumped in fright as the voice boomed out of the darkness.

'Wh-what?'

A torch suddenly flared and there, emerging from behind one of the pillars was a tall, gaunt figure with sparse, straggly hair and wild eyes. He stumped forward, his wooden leg thumping the flagstones dully.

'Grume!' exclaimed Vane.

'Wh-who?' Vinny mumbled, still trying to get over the shock.

'Hello, Vane,' said the owner of the Café in the Crypt, holding out his gnarled hand to the little werewolf. 'Good to see you again. Have to say I was getting a mite lonely hiding down here in these catacombs.'

Chapter Thirty-four

With Joe still clinging to his back, Corpus and the others turned off the slippery cobbles and into the depths of a pillared doorway. A signal was rapped on the door, which was opened almost immediately. The vampires swept through and into a shuttered room lit by a single candle.

Joe peered over Corpus's shoulder at the figure who had admitted them – a young woman dressed in a high-necked, indigo-velvet gown. Her hair was jet-black and hung thickly over her shoulders, framing a pale, angular face with large, dark eyes. A strange face, thought Joe – part beautiful and part unsettling.

As the vampires took off their hoods Joe saw her face light up with pleasure and the points of her eye teeth flash white as she smiled.

'Muesli!' she cried. 'Welcome back! And Corpus too –' She then gazed directly into Joe's eyes – 'who has a passenger, I see.'

Joe slid to the ground and Muesli introduced him.

'Joe . . . this is Sable, sister of my friends here, Krazul and Darceth.'

'I'm truly delighted to meet you, Joe,' said Sable, bowing. 'Alchema told me all about your bravery last time you were here in Eyetooth.'

Joe felt himself blush and Alchema stepped forward with a smile, laying her hand on his shoulder.

'You're embarrassing the lad, Sable,' she murmured.

Looking at Krazul and Darceth, Joe immediately saw the family resemblance. Both had their sister's disconcerting good looks although Krazul was a head taller than his brother. He was about to reply when a sudden wave of weakness washed over him and he felt his knees buckle.

Corpus was first to react, seizing him by

the arms and sitting him on a low stool.

'A reviving glass for Joe, Sable?' he said. 'Poor lad thought he was a goner back there in the birdcage.'

I did, thought Joe. It was like being in a nightmare where you try to wake up but can't.

Sable lifted a silver jug from a nearby table, poured a small measure of dark liquid into a silver goblet.

'Sip this,' she said. 'It'll do you good.'

As Joe hesitated and peered at the contents doubtfully, Sable laughed.

'It's not blood, if that's what you're thinking, Joe. It's an elixir made from plants and herbs that Grume gave me. Very reviving. Go on . . . drink.'

Joe trusted these friends of Muesli so he drank – and as the liquid went down he felt a warm, relaxing glow spread through his body. Feeling his strength rapidly returning, he smiled up at the young vampire.

'Thanks,' he replied gratefully. 'I feel better already.'

Muesli squatted down beside him and the others gathered round.

'Better enough to tell us what happened?'

Joe quickly recounted his story – from the

time he and Vinny pursued Anthonia into the mountain, to Anthonia's wounding of one of the vampires and her disappearance.

'What a terrible thing for her to do,' growled Corpus to Joe. 'Imagine leaving you on your own in Eyetooth!'

'Yes . . .' mused Alchema, 'very selfish. She seems to be obsessed with this notion of being a vampire hunter.'

'And has made her presence felt already,' added Darceth.

'Indeed,' agreed his brother, his eyes twinkling. 'At least one of Fibula's men got the *point*!'

Muesli smiled briefly then sighed.

'Trouble is, we have no way of knowing if she is still free or has already been captured.'

'What about Dad and Vane, Muesli?' asked Joe anxiously. 'Do you think they're all right?'

'If anyone knows the tunnels it's Vane,' replied Muesli with a reassuring smile. 'He'll get your father out, don't worry. Once he finds that you and Anthonia have gone he'll make sure Vinny is safe before coming to Eyetooth to find out what's happened here.'

'The girl ... Anthonia ...' Sable interjected, 'will, I am afraid, have to look to herself. Any search for her would mean delay, and would play into Fibula's hands. My feeling is that we should act now to topple Fibula. A delay could be fatal.'

Muesli stood up and gazed at her, undisguised admiration in his eyes.

'You're right, Sable. We must act now.' He looked at Alchema. 'How many are in jail altogether?'

'Eleven, I believe,' answered Alchema.

'So, if we succeed in freeing them we will be seventeen.'

'Eighteen!' Joe piped up. 'Don't forget me!'

Corpus grinned but shook his head.

'You're very brave, Joe,' he said, 'but you'll have to stay out of this fight, I'm afraid. It's not for you.' He turned back to Alchema.

'We'll have seventeen to combat ... how many?'

Alchema made a wry face.

'Around forty, I would estimate. Although,' she went on, 'some of those may not have the stomach for a battle. Bray is still at liberty, of course, and she is on our side.'

'The odds are still heavily stacked in Fibula's favour,' Muesli said. 'So,' he paused and gazed at them all, 'we should try to free our friends now . . . immediately . . . before he can organize his henchmen. We have a slight start on him – let's use it.'

Alchema shook her head and smiled at the young vampire.

'I still cannot get used to the change in you, Muesli. From fun-lover to leader. Remarkable!'

'I always knew that Muesli had hidden depths,' said Sable, her dark eyes twinkling.

Muesli returned her look with a grin.

'So we go now?' asked Darceth, his brother nodding eagerly in agreement.

Muesli stretched out his hand, palm down.

'Now,' he said.

Sable walked forward and laid her hand on his.

'Now,' she said.

One by one, Alchema, Corpus, Darceth and Krazul did the same until they formed a circle in the centre of the candlelit room.

Joe felt like pinching himself – here he was back in Eyetooth watching his vampire friends pledge to fight, not only to preserve the good in Eyetooth but to protect humans from a vampire onslaught. The thought sent shivers down his spine.

'It's agreed,' said Muesli. 'Tonight we do battle with Fibula.'

Corpus grinned. He lifted his tousled head and squared his massive shoulders, taking a deep breath as if readying himself for action. The candlelight caught the wild gleam in his eyes.

'Just let me at them,' he growled.

Chapter Thirty-five

'No one will disturb us here,' Bray said quietly as she guided Anthonia through a low doorway and into a dark corridor, locking the door behind her. 'This is my home. Fibula's minions have already searched for me here so will never dream that I would be foolhardy enough to return.'

At the end of the corridor there was a small, curtained room. They entered and Bray lit a candle. 'Now,' she said, laying the crossbow on a chair and turning to the girl, 'I want the truth. You can tell me of your own free will or I can extract it from you by a simple and painless method.'

'You mean by using *the voice?*' asked Anthonia.

'Ah,' said Bray, startled. 'You know about that, do you?'

'My great-grandmother's diary speaks of it,' answered Anthonia. 'She was immune to it, as are all great vampire hunters. No vampire could master her just by using their stupid, hypnotic chant.'

'Not so stupid, my dear,' responded Bray, frowning. 'Can be jolly useful, you know.' She regarded the girl thoughtfully for a moment, then said, 'So, you believe that you too are immune to the voice?'

'You want to try me?' demanded Anthonia defiantly.

Bray smiled and scratched her tangled green curls.

'Could but I won't,' she boomed. 'Too tiring.' She dropped her voice and gazed into Anthonia's eyes.

'I'm banking on the fact that, despite being a foolish girl, you are not a liar at heart.'

Anthonia held the gaze.

'I'm not a liar,' she said.

'Then tell me,' asked Bray, 'who else came to Eyetooth with you?'

Anthonia stared into the dark green eyes for a few seconds before answering.

Bray sat immobile, her face like stone

as the girl recounted what had happened.

When Anthonia finished, Bray simply turned away from her and began pacing the room, eyes staring fixedly into the distance as she talked aloud to herself.

'Muesli and Corpus back . . . Joe loose. Fibula bound to find out . . . not good, not good . . .'

A sudden tapping at the window that lay behind the heavy drapes startled them.

As Bray snuffed the candle they heard a faint, insistent whispering.

In the thick darkness Anthonia was dimly aware of the countess's shape moving towards the curtains.

Quietly, Bray pulled the drapes wide and threw open the long window.

Anthonia saw two dark figures clamber over the sill. Instinctively she backed away from them.

Bray drew the curtains again and quickly relit the candle.

In the first flare of light Anthonia saw both faces and gasped.

'It's you!'

'Anthonia!' Vinny cried, astonished. He looked quickly around the room. 'Where's Joe? I thought . . .'

'I gather that you are Joe's father,' said Bray, interrupting.

'That's right,' replied Vinny agitatedly, turning to stare at her. 'Vane tells me you are Countess Bray.'

'I am.' She held up her hand to stop Vinny continuing. 'Joe is not here, Vinny. You will find out why in a moment. I know some of the story from Anthonia but just now I want to hear the rest of it.'

Bray turned her attention to Vane.

'The news, Vane . . . quickly.'

In an urgent, earnest tone the little werewolf swiftly told her how he and Vinny had found their way into the catacombs beneath the Café in the Crypt and about their meeting with Grume.

'I was taking Vinny back to the tunnels to meet up with Joe and . . .' he glanced disapprovingly at Anthonia, 'this girl . . . when we had to hide from approaching vampires. Turned out it was Spitz and Horba. They were talking as they passed; furious, they were – and we found out two things: that Joe had miraculously escaped from them, and that they were off to warn Fibula.' The little werewolf blinked nervously. 'I-I decided I had to tell someone.

Your house was nearest and I just took a chance.' He glanced at Vinny. 'Vinny insisted on coming.'

'I just assumed that you and Joe were together when he escaped from the vampires,' Vinny said to Anthonia. 'I expected him to be here when I saw you. So how did you two become separated?'

The girl looked shamefaced.

'It's my fault,' she said. 'I came up to Eyetooth, forcing Joe to follow. When we got here I-I ran away from him.'

Vinny looked at her incredulously and Bray laid a reassuring hand on his arm.

'At least we know that Joe is still free,' she said quietly.

Vinny bit his lip and shook his head fretfully.

'We have to find him,' he muttered. 'We have to!'

'Yes,' agreed Vane. 'We must. And not only for the boy's own safety. Once Fibula finds out that Joe is here he'll put two and two together – he'll assume Count Muesli and Count Corpus are back. He'll gather his forces to crush them once and for all. We'll all be done for.'

Bray looked thoughtful.

'Yes ... and we are outnumbered by Fibula's vampires,' she said. 'Two to one – and that's counting our supporters who are in jail.'

'Can't you get reinforcements from somewhere?' asked Vinny anxiously. 'They could help us find Joe.'

'Well,' Bray mused, 'there are other vampires, of course, but they are very old. They keep their own counsel and have never become involved in the politics of Eyetooth.'

'Surely they can see that Fibula is a bad lot?' protested Vinny. 'Couldn't they be persuaded?'

Bray frowned.

'Perhaps,' she said.

Vane tugged at Bray's sleeve.

'Er ... what about asking Count Zircon?' he suggested. 'He's the oldest and, some say, the wisest vampire in Eyetooth. If he can be persuaded, then the others might too.'

'Good thinking, Vane,' exclaimed Bray. 'You've got a clever head on those furry shoulders of yours.' She hurried to the door. 'We will all go.' She looked across at Anthonia, who sat, brows furrowed, staring at the floor. 'Including you, Anthonia. Like

182

it or not you are involved in our struggle now. And, like it or not, there *are* good vampires in Eyetooth.' Her eyes fell on Anthonia's crossbow lying on the chair. 'We'll leave your weapon behind. You might . . . accidentally . . . injure one of our friends with it. If there is to be a battle for Eyetooth it will be fought hand-to-hand – with ferocity, strength, skill and cunning. And may good prevail.'

Chapter Thirty-six

Fibula stared at Spitz and Horba in disbelief.

'The boy . . . *here*?' His pale, thin face contorted in fury. Spinning round, he snatched a goblet from the table and hurled it against the wall where it smashed into a thousand pieces, leaving tiny, bright shards of crystal and dark-red drops of rats' blood spread over the flagstones. 'And you let him escape? Fools! *Fools!*'

The irony of this was not lost on Spitz and Horba. Barely half an hour ago they had berated other vampires in much the same way for running from the vampire hunter.

'He-he disappeared, Count Fibula,' Horba muttered. 'There must be a secret exit from the birdcage.'

'Impossible!' screamed Fibula. 'No one has ever escaped from there. He was taken from right under your noses!'

The leader of the council turned away from his two henchmen and began to pace up and down in front of the great fireplace, staring at the floor, bony hands clasped behind his back under his swirling black cloak.

Behind him Ichor scurried out of the darkness and quietly began to sweep up the crystal shards and rats' blood.

Fibula stopped pacing. As he looked up, his two henchmen saw that the fury had gone and was replaced by a look of cold certainty.

'Muesli and Corpus have returned,' he said. 'This is the only explanation for the boy's presence. And if the boy is here, then his father or others of his family will be here too. They must have come with the vampire hunter.' He leant towards them, holding their eyes in his gimlet gaze, and continued, his voice low and harsh. 'Their purpose is to defeat me, that is clear. And the only way

185

they can do that is by having a credible number of vampires on their side.' His voice became icy as he emphasized his next words. '*Which means that they will have to free the rebels who are in jail.*'

Spitz and Horba shared a quick, startled glance.

'What are your orders?' said Spitz.

Fibula thought for a moment then looked at Spitz.

'How long will it take to assemble those under my command?' he asked, glancing at the ancient long-case clock in the shadows.

'About thirty minutes,' replied Spitz. 'Horba and I will make sure of it. We know where the patrols should be.'

'Then tell them to assemble in my court-yard at midnight.'

Chapter Thirty-seven

The rain had stopped and now a thin white mist drifted down over the roofs and rock pinnacles of Eyetooth. A silver-grey sheen like the breath of a thousand ghosts touched walls and battlements.

Inside Count Zircon's study the ruddy light from a blazing fire flickered over heavy furniture, ornate bookcases and velvet drapes. A narrow staircase curved up to a small, book-lined gallery overflowing with aged documents and parchments. In the shadows beyond the firelight loomed strange astronomical instruments and an ancient globe of the world mounted on a carved wooden frame. Maps of the heavens hung on the dark walls.

Bray sat at Zircon's bidding and, leaning forward, gazed into her ancient host's eyes.

'Thank you for seeing me, Count Zircon,' she said. 'I have come to ask you for help.'

'Help?' Zircon arched a white eyebrow and regarded Bray calmly. 'What kind of help?'

Bray hesitated for a second.

'It is said that you do not like Fibula, Count Zircon. Is that true?'

'It is no secret,' replied Zircon. 'But I have never opposed him in any way.' He shook his head slowly and gazed into the fire. 'I do not interfere. I do not take sides.'

'There are others – the older vampires – who think like you,' stated Bray quietly. 'Is that not so?'

The old vampire looked at her pensively, his deep-set eyes glittering red in the fire-light.

'It is.'

Bray took a deep breath.

'I believe the time has come to take sides, Count Zircon. We vampires have become used to living here in our safe haven. We have ceased preying on humankind. We are content. Many of us want that way of life to continue and . . .' she leant forward, glaring fiercely, 'it *would* continue if not for Fibula! He has stirred up the old, forgotten blood-lust. If he silences all opposition here then the attacks on humans will begin again. We must not let this happen. In the end Eyetooth's secret will be destroyed . . . and so will we. I believe that he must be removed. *Now.*'

Zircon sighed and stared once more into the flames.

'I thought it would come to this,' he murmured. 'I knew that sooner or later I would have to choose. And in a way I am glad.' He lifted his gaze to Bray. 'I am ancient,' he said. 'Almost five hundred years old. Older by a hundred years than the oldest vampires in Eyetooth. In my younger days I was a warrior, a battler, a victor. For the last two centuries I have taken no part in any struggle, preferring to live a quiet life. But recently, as I have watched Fibula turn the very air of Eyetooth sour with greed and distrust, I knew my quiet life was ending.' His eyes glimmered. 'Tonight I return to the ways of my youth. Tonight,' he said, his voice growing stronger, sharper, 'I return to battle.'

Bray's eyes were shining.

'I hoped you would say that,' she said. 'But, Count, time is of the essence. We must have more supporters if Fibula's plan is to be foiled. Muesli and Corpus have returned and now we need as many on our side as possible.'

There was a short silence as Count Zircon regarded her thoughtfully.

'I will contact my friends,' he replied at last. 'Old vampires but strong in heart and mind.'

Agitatedly Bray got to her feet.

'But,' she protested, 'we need them to-night, Count Zircon. We cannot wait until messages are sent around Eyetooth.'

The old vampire regarded her with amusement.

'In my long years I have learnt many things,' he said. 'One of the most important is how to make the *mind* do the work of the *body*.' He gestured to her chair. 'Sit again, Bray,' he said. 'I will summon my friends. They will not be long. I have made my decision but it is up to them to make theirs.'

'But, Count . . .' Bray began, flustered, only to be halted by the old vampire's raised hand.

'Patience, Bray,' he murmured.

He crossed his hands on his lap and, as the countess reluctantly resumed her seat, he leant his head back against the faded velvet of his chair and closed his eyes.

As Bray watched the thin, noble figure in his flowing grey robes she saw a calm, serene expression suffuse his time-ravaged features and sensed he had entered a deep trance.

In the room there was no sound save for the whispering made by the burning logs as they occasionally shifted in their bed of glowing cinders.

Chapter Thirty-eight

Joe peered out over a wall that linked two crumbling pillars and stared across the empty square towards the jail. The light from a burning brazier by the jail door glimmered through the thin curtains of cold mist that blew slowly across the bleak space. Joe shivered inside his zipped-up jacket. Alongside him hunched Muesli and the other vampires.

'Still no one, Muesli,' he whispered.

Muesli frowned.

'No . . . I thought there might have been more coming and going, giving us a chance to rush in while the door was open. But no one's gone in or come out in the last ten minutes.'

'What we need is a battering ram,' grumbled Corpus quietly.

An idea had been forming in Joe's mind and now he decided to share it.

'Muesli,' he whispered, tugging at the young vampire's sleeve. 'I've been think-ing . . . what about using me as a decoy?'

'A decoy?' repeated Muesli, startled, as the others turned to listen.

'Yeah,' Joe went on, 'supposing I was to wander into the square . . . as if I was lost. Don't you think one of the jailors would come out and try to grab me? If that happened you could all rush in.'

Corpus grinned in admiration.

'A brave plan, Joe,' he murmured. 'If a tad dangerous.'

'Too dangerous,' whispered Sable. 'The vampire who comes out might harm you, Joe.'

'Yes . . .' murmured Muesli thoughtfully, 'but the decoy idea might not be such a bad one after all.' He looked at the vampires round him, then said, 'You don't like Spitz much, do you, Corpus?'

The big vampire's mouth twisted in a grimace.

'Not much,' he replied softly.

'Although I've heard you do a fair impression of his screeching voice . . .' Muesli said, a ghost of a smile on his lips, 'and you're just as big as him,' he went on before Corpus could reply.

Sable smiled.

'I think I see what you're suggesting,' she breathed. 'You mean – have Corpus pretend he is Spitz?'

'Exactly,' replied Muesli.

Corpus chuckled softly.

'Yes . . . in this mist and with my hood up they might not be able to tell the difference.'

'It might work,' agreed Krazul slowly.

'It would *definitely* work, Muesli,' whispered Joe, 'if Corpus, as Spitz, had *me* with him . . . *as a prisoner*. That would fool them! They'd be sure to open the door then, wouldn't they?'

'Joe's plan is a good one,' said Sable thoughtfully. 'I think we should allow him to help. We know he's proved himself to be quick and brave.'

The others quietly whispered their agreement and Joe felt good that he was going to be able to assist in such a positive way. He almost felt like an honorary vampire.

'All right, Joe,' said Muesli. He patted Joe's shoulder and looked around at his friends. 'We will cut round and wait in the alley. Corpus will storm across the square in full view of the window, bawling out that he has the boy and for them to open up. As soon as they open the door we will rush in.' He looked at Joe with concern. 'You stay back by the door of the jail, Joe. If anything goes wrong . . . run!'

'I will,' replied Joe, his heart beginning to beat faster at the thought of the action to come.

The mist, still thin and transparent, drifted slowly across the square, turning from pearly-white to yellow as it eddied round the burning brazier.

Joe and Corpus waited tensely in the shadow of a doorway for Muesli's signal from the alley opposite. When it came, Corpus gripped Joe by the arm and winked before pulling up his hood.

'Here we go, Joe!' he whispered, his eyes twinkling in the deep shadows of the cowl. 'You all right? Ready for a bit of play-acting?'

Joe took a deep breath and smiled.

'I'm ready.'

Corpus squared his shoulders, cleared his throat and strode out into the open, dragging a struggling Joe beside him.

'Open up!' he shouted harshly in Spitz's arrogant, strident tones. 'D'you hear in there? Open up, blast your eyes!'

'Let . . . me . . . go!' yelled Joe, squirming theatrically in the big vampire's grip.

From under his cowl Corpus saw faces appear momentarily at the barred window of the jail. Come on, come on, open the door, he thought as he reached the middle of the square. I don't want to get too close.

'Open, I say!' he bawled, gesticulating angrily with his free hand. 'What are you waiting for? I have the boy!'

The sudden rattling of bolts being drawn cut across his shouting and Corpus had to stop himself from smiling with relief as he thought, it's working.

The door to the jail swung open and two figures appeared on the threshold.

'Spitz –' one of them began, then gasped in shock as Muesli and the others suddenly appeared from the shadows and leapt on him and his companion.

As they all disappeared into the jail in a

thresh of arms and legs Corpus let go of Joe's arm and sprinted forward.

'Keep a lookout, Joe!' he cried.

The big vampire swept through the doorway and into the jail's office, tensed for action. On the floor to his left he saw that Darceth and Krazul had subdued one of the jailors while, to his right, Muesli and Sable had overcome the second. He felt a pang of disappointment at having missed the fun but in that instant a movement at the back of the room caught his attention. *The connecting door between the office and the cells was closing.*

Corpus moved like lightning. He charged across the room and hurled his massive shoulder against the door just before it shut completely. The heavy door recoiled explosively and struck whoever was on the other side a jarring, violent blow. There was a sharp cry followed by a thump and, looking down, Corpus saw a limp hand flop into view. The door had only swung inwards a little but the speeding weight of Corpus's bulk had sent it crashing into the fleeing figure with the force of a cannonball. Squeezing through the gap into the small hallway between the office and the cells, the big vampire saw the unconscious figure of the third jailor stretched out on the floor. In the slack grip of his hand was a large ring from which hung a number of keys.

'I'll have these, matey,' murmured Corpus.

Chapter Thirty-nine

Bray watched, fascinated, as Count Zircon's telepathic summons was answered.

It took only a few minutes for the first vampires, Count and Countess Interra, to arrive.

They swept in regally, their haughty old faces severe, their fierce bright eyes undimmed. After bowing to Zircon and Bray without a word, they quietly moved to the centre of the room where they stood immobile, swathed in their long, black silk cloaks.

Now, ten minutes on from that first, dramatic entrance, fifteen vampires stood solemnly in Zircon's study. Everyone had greeted Zircon and Bray with a bow, then moved away to join the other arrivals. All were now deep in muted conversation as they waited for the final participants to enter.

Bray wondered how long she should delay fetching Vane, Vinny and Anthonia. She also wondered how many more of the older vampires would come. Zircon moved away from the group and approached her.

'Two more, Bray,' he murmured. 'When they arrive we will debate.'

Bray felt she could wait no longer to inform Zircon about Vane and the others.

'I have something to tell you, Count,' she began, but a sudden commotion in the hall interrupted her and made every head turn.

The door was abruptly thrown open and Vane, Vinny and Anthonia were ushered in, followed by two elderly, and very angry, vampires.

The newcomers confronted Bray.

'What is the meaning of this, Countess Bray?' demanded the first, a small, wrinkled vampire with tied-back grey hair. 'We caught them skulking about outside. They say they are with you.'

Countess Bray made a wry face but held

her head up proudly as she turned to Count Zircon. 'I feel a bit of an ass, Count,' she barked. 'Should have told you about them right away. But what's done's done. Can't be helped now. Allow me to explain.'

She looked around the gathering. 'I came here tonight to ask Count Zircon for help in removing Fibula,' she said briskly. 'I would have come anyway but it also happened that I encountered these three.' She gestured to each one in turn. 'Vane you know . . . brave and loyal. Vinny, a human, you may have heard about. He was last here in Eyetooth over a month ago. Muesli helped him and his family escape from Fibula. Vinny is searching for his son, Joe, who came to Eyetooth with him tonight but is now lost. Anthonia . . .' she hesitated slightly before going on, 'regards herself as a vampire hunter.' There were startled gasps from the old vampires.

'A vampire hunter?' cried Count Interra incredulously. 'Surely not, Bray. She's a mere girl!'

Anthonia was stung. She felt her face colour and before she could stop herself she cried out petulantly, 'I am not a *mere* girl! I came close to destroying one of your kind tonight – and my great-grandmother, Beatrice Harrington, wasn't much older than me when she destroyed more than ten vampires a hundred years ago!'

Most of the vampires did not react to the name but a few did – and one of those was Count Zircon.

'Beatrice!' he hissed, amazed. 'You? You are Beatrice Harrington's great-grand-daughter?'

'Yes!' replied Anthonia hotly. She stared at Zircon belligerently then, as she saw the look of wonder on his face, her anger subsided.

The old vampire slowly shook his head.

'Now that I really look at you I see,' he whispered. 'You are the living image of your great-grandmother. Your voice, even, is the same . . . and your hot temper.'

Anthonia blinked rapidly, confused and disorientated.

'You *met* my great-grandmother? *Talked* to her? But how could you? She vowed to destroy all vampires! She would have destroyed *you*! I read all her journals.'

The old vampires moved closer, fascinated and intrigued by this exchange.

Count Zircon smiled kindly.

'All her journals, Anthonia?' he said quietly. 'You read all of them?'

'Yes.'

'Did you read why she ceased hunting vampires?'

Anthonia looked puzzled.

'She didn't write down anything about that,' she muttered.

'Ah, but she did,' answered Zircon.

'When?' demanded Anthonia.

'When she was here as my guest,' replied the old vampire. 'Almost one hundred years ago to the day.'

Anthonia gasped and little hushed murmurs and whispers of astonishment spread round the room.

'She came here?' said Anthonia hoarsely.

'At my invitation,' replied Zircon. 'She knew that, as a guest, she would not be harmed. The vampire code is very strict about that.'

'But it's a code which Fibula does not live by,' interjected Bray gruffly, and a murmur of agreement came from the gathering.

'No,' Zircon went on, holding Anthonia's gaze. 'That is true. Fibula and his like care nothing for the ancient vampire code of honour.'

Bray glanced at Anthonia triumphantly.

'You see, girl?' she murmured. 'As I said – not all vampires are the same.'

Zircon turned and looked into the fire for a moment.

'I will tell you,' he said finally, still staring into the flames. 'I met Beatrice the last time I left Eyetooth. I had journeyed from the mountain to meet a friend I knew was fleeing from the vampire hunters. I was to guide my friend here – to safety.' He sighed and shook his head at the memory. 'I arrived at our meeting place only to find that my friend had just been slain . . . by Beatrice.'

Anthonia's eyes widened and there was an angry murmur from the vampires.

'What happened then?' she whispered.

Count Zircon turned to face her again.

'I could have killed her easily,' he said quietly. 'But I knew that revenge was not the answer. I knew that if I killed Beatrice then the other vampire hunters would find out and pursue me all the way back to Eyetooth. I would have signed a death warrant for all those that exist here. I would have betrayed them. I chose instead to forgive her, to talk to her, to invite her here so that she could see for herself that there were many vampires who only wanted to be left in peace. I asked her if she would accept our right to be left alone in our secret refuge – and finally she agreed.' Count Zircon walked slowly to a bookcase by the fire and extracted a thin, leather-bound book, which he handed to Anthonia. 'This is your great-grandmother's last 'vampire' journal, Anthonia. Read it. You will see how she agreed not only to leave us in peace but also to keep our secret forever. She swore that my friend was the last vampire she would kill. I believe she kept that promise.'

For a long moment nothing was said – the only noise in the room the soft rustle of turning pages as Anthonia, ashen-faced, leafed through her great-grandmother's last journal.

At last she raised her head and looked at Count Zircon.

'I see I was wrong,' she whispered. 'I've been stupid.'

Countess Bray patted her arm.

'No, my dear!' she boomed, shattering the quiet in the room. 'You've been very courageous! It's honourable to admit that you were wrong.'

Anthonia threw a grateful glance at Bray then turned to Zircon.

'My great-grandmother kept her word and your secret,' she said firmly. 'I found her other journals, clothes, silver pistol and crossbow in a locked box in the attic of her old house. She told no one of her time as a vampire hunter, not even her husband and children.'

'The vampires your great-grandmother hated most were the greedy ones, Anthonia,' Count Zircon went on. 'Those who, even after satisfying their need for blood, continued to attack humans just to show how powerful they were. Fibula was one of that kind before he retreated to Eyetooth – and now his greed and desire for power have returned.'

'He must be stopped,' barked Bray.

Vane, gripping his umbrella tightly in front of him, spoke up at last.

'He must – he really must,' said the little werewolf agitatedly. 'Count Muesli and Count Corpus and their friends can't be left to fight Fibula alone.'

Anthonia stared at the old vampires.

'I understand now that not all vampires are alike,' she said quietly, 'thanks to

Countess Bray and Count Zircon. Will you join with them to fight Fibula?'

Zircon and the old vampires did not respond, merely gazing at her with hooded eyes, their expressions hard to fathom. At last Zircon turned to his friends.

'Indeed,' he said. 'That is my question. Will you?' He looked slowly around, searching every face, reading the emotions behind the glittering old eyes. The aged vampires held his gaze and, one by one, each nodded imperceptibly. No words were needed.

'So ... we have agreement,' he said gravely. 'We will help Muesli rid Eyetooth of Fibula and his like forever.'

'Thank you,' replied Bray simply.

The small vampire with the tied-back grey hair stepped forward.

'As we came here we saw Fibula leave his castle at the head of a large group of vampires,' he said. 'They turned down the alley that leads to the jail. He obviously plans to lie in wait for Muesli. He and Corpus are bound to try and free their friends at some point.'

'Fibula hopes to catch Muesli in the act,' murmured Count Interra.

Count Zircon held his old head up

proudly, a fierce glint in his eyes. 'It seems that our battleground has been chosen for us. Let us go . . . quickly!'

Chapter Forty

All the cell doors lay open as Muesli and his friends looked after the freed prisoners. A flagon of rats' blood and bottles of Fangola had been found in the office and cups were being passed among the thankful vampires.

'Been here for three weeks,' gasped Raggar, one of Muesli's friends, as he hungrily drained a glass of Fangola. 'Thought I'd never get out. I tell you, you're a sight for sore eyes, Muesli.'

'Yes, thank you, Muesli,' said Countess Plaza from the doorway, an empty cup of rats' blood in her hand. 'Your return to Eyetooth is most welcome.' She put down the cup and massaged her wrists. 'I think I'll carry the mark of Fibula's manacles with me for a while,' she murmured, wincing.

'Rest and gather strength, both of you,' Muesli replied. 'The real struggle against Fibula has just begun.'

Countess Plaza scowled.

'The sooner Eyetooth is rid of him the better,' she muttered darkly.

'I'll second that,' said old Vennel bitterly as he hobbled past, rubbing his back. 'They destroyed my coffincar on his orders.'

'Don't worry, Vennel, I'll help you to rebuild it,' said Muesli.

The old vampire smiled his thanks.

In the corridor Muesli met Alchema coming out of one of the cells.

'The three jailors are safely tied up, Muesli,' she said, 'and all eleven captives appear to be well enough, although a few are weak. They need to rest and recover before taking on Fibula ... but there's really no time.'

'I know, Alchema,' responded Muesli. 'We have to –'

The door at the end of the corridor burst open and Joe rushed in, eyes wide. 'There's a big bunch of vampires coming across the square with Fibula, Muesli!' he cried. 'I've bolted the door!'

'Good work, Joe,' said Muesli as he and Alchema ran past him and into the office, joined quickly by Corpus, Darceth, Krazul and Sable as they rushed from the cells.

Muesli peered cautiously out into the square from the side of the jail's heavily barred window while Alchema and Krazul lifted up the ancient oak bar from the floor and quietly slid it into place across the doorway.

'They're almost here!' he cried hoarsely. 'A large group, maybe forty.'

Darceth blew out the solitary candle as a sudden pounding began on the door, followed by strident bellowing.

'Open up, jailor! Count Fibula is here!' The voice was harsh and arrogant.

'Spitz!' whispered Muesli to Corpus, and the big vampire's lip curled in distaste.

The pounding stopped and there was silence for a few seconds before it began again, more fiercely this time.

'Open immediately, do you hear?' came an angry roar from Spitz.

Faces clustered outside the window, trying to peer through the latticed bars

211

and small, grimy windowpanes into the darkened interior.

Muesli, Corpus, Joe and the others slid into the deepest shadows while the freed prisoners crowded into the hallway between the cells and the office, standing silent and still.

They heard Spitz bawling, 'Try the side door!' and immediately faces turned away from the window as some of Fibula's vampires headed for the alley.

'Don't worry, it's locked and barred,' hissed Sable to Muesli and Corpus as they looked across the darkened office towards the hallway. 'I checked when we arrived.'

A sudden rattling and thumping from the door in the small hallway was followed by loud, echoing curses in the alley.

'What are you going to do, Muesli?' whispered Joe, crawling from behind the table to crouch beside the window with the young vampire. 'We're trapped in here. Are you going to go out and fight?'

Muesli sighed.

'This is not how I saw it happening, Joe,' he replied. 'We're outnumbered two to one and some of our friends are weak. But . . .' He grimaced. 'What's the use of pretending we're not here? They'll find out eventually and then we'll have to fight.'

'Been forced into it so let's do it,' rumbled Corpus, cracking his knuckles agitatedly.

'I agree with Corpus,' hissed Raggar, squeezing through the group of vampires in the hall and stepping into the room.

'Are you strong enough for a battle, Ragg?' asked Muesli with concern.

'Do or die, Mooz,' replied his friend quietly, and the vampires behind him murmured their agreement.

Corpus raised his head slightly.

'Gone a bit quiet out there,' he murmured. 'What are they up to?'

Krazul stole over to the door and put his ear to a crack in the ancient wood.

'Sounds like they're having a discussion,' he whispered.

The next moment the vampires directly outside the window were roughly pushed aside and a burning brand was thrust against the bars.

From their hiding place Muesli and his friends saw a large face appear at the window. Although the face was indistinct through the grime, Corpus recognized it immediately.

'That's Spitz,' he hissed.

The light from the burning brand didn't penetrate far into the office, only succeeding in casting its sickly yellow glow on to a small part of the floor.

'Can't see much,' Spitz's voice rasped from outside.

'Doesn't matter. I know they're in there. I can sense it!' came an icy snarl in return.

'Fibula,' Muesli whispered to Corpus.

The harsh voice of Fibula rang out again.

'Now!'

Instantly a volley of rocks came hurtling at the windows. Some rebounded from the bars with a sharp clamour but others smashed right through the windowpanes then clattered across the flagstones, sending shards of glass flying into the darkened office. These were followed a fraction of a second later by the flying forms of half a dozen torches, propelled through the jagged gaps to the accompaniment of wild screams from Fibula's vampires.

Five of the flaming brands fell harmlessly on to the centre of the flagstoned floor but one glanced off the crouching figure of Corpus, dropping on to the folds of his cloak, which was bunched on the floor behind him.

The big vampire jerked to the side, swiped the burning torch on to the stone flags then began to beat at his smouldering cloak.

Joe now saw with horror that Corpus's long, tangled mass of black hair was on fire – a bright crackle of small flames spreading quickly up the thick tendrils that hung over the big vampire's collar.

Muesli cried out a warning but Joe was first to react. Leaping up, he wrenched off his jacket and threw it against the back of Corpus's head, smothering the blaze in the thick fabric.

Startled, Corpus twisted round and managed a quick, rueful grin as he realized what Joe had done.

'Quick thinking, Joe,' he said, dabbing at the back of his head as the acrid smell of burnt hair filled the room. 'I'm not hurt – although another second or two and I reckon my head would have been like a roasted nut.'

The office was once more plunged into darkness as the freed prisoners quickly picked up the burning torches and removed them to the cells.

215

Outside, the screeching of the besieging vampires stopped abruptly and everyone in the office heard Fibula's hate-filled shout cut through the silence.

'Now I know who I am dealing with. *Muesli! Corpus!*' There was a pause and when Fibula spoke again his voice had dropped to a seething hiss, full of scorn and venom. 'I've been waiting for your return, *traitors*, but I expected a harder fight than this! Although I'm not complaining, oh no! Far from it. I'm delighted that you have made it easy for me – walked into a nice little trap of your own choosing. And with the *vampire hunter* too! Such a shame! I won't have the honour of making his acquaintance before you all perish together.' He began to laugh softly and the laughter was taken up by his followers, quietly at first, then growing in volume until the air shook with their shrieks and howls of mirth.

Chapter Forty-one

The mist was becoming thicker and foggy veils shrouded the narrow streets.

Having hurried ahead on a scouting mission, Vane now dashed back along the twisting, misty lane towards the group of old vampires led by Bray and Zircon. He waved his umbrella frantically.

'Fibula's at the jail with dozens of his henchmen,' he gasped as he reached them. 'I think he's going to set fire to the place. They've got barrels of lamp oil and they're rolling them up to the door.'

'Muesli must be in there,' boomed Bray. 'Only explanation.'

'Do you think Joe's with them?'

exclaimed Vinny anxiously, turning to Zircon.

'Possibly,' replied the aged count. 'Come, there's no time to lose.'

'Yes, come on, come on,' cried Vane, running ahead for a few paces then back again just as a dog would. He waved his tattered umbrella in the air like a flag. 'Hurry! Hurry!'

As one, the old vampires surged forward and Vinny found he had to trot to keep up with them. For all their aged limbs, they seemed to be able to cover the ground quite speedily.

Not speedily enough for Anthonia, however. She had been keeping pace but now suddenly broke free and flew away from them down the alley towards the jail.

'Stop!' Bray yelled, taken by surprise, but Anthonia ignored her and a moment later turned the corner and was out of sight.

Chapter Forty-two

Anthonia was running so fast she found herself in the jailhouse square before she knew it. Fibula's vampires were gathered in a swarming, noisy group on the other side of the square, about fifty metres away from her. Realizing they hadn't seen her yet, she quickly halted, threw off her rucksack and withdrew two stake-darts before slinging the bag on to her back again. Taking a deep breath and squaring her shoulders, she pulled the brim of her hat down and gripped a stake in each hand.

'I am the vampire hunter!' she bellowed, forcing her voice to cut through the snarling hubbub at the jail.

A few startled heads turned and stared in astonishment. Two vampires halted in the act of tipping up barrels of lamp oil by the jailhouse door. Seconds later the bustle and noise at the jail had ceased and every head was looking her way.

'I am the vampire hunter!' she shouted again fiercely, angrily. 'Which one of you is Fibula?'

As Anthonia watched, out of the throng stepped a vampire, his long black cloak thrown over his shoulders and fastened at the neck by a gold clasp. He was followed closely by two others – one a hulking bald brute, the other short and swarthy with a thick moustache. The leading vampire was of medium height, his grey hair hanging in tendrils on either side of his thin, pale face, his red eyes glittering beneath drawn brows.

Anthonia's first impression was that this was an unremarkable figure but, as she stared at the hard face with its high fore-head and cruel mouth she quickly realized its power. She could almost feel the menace in the gimlet stare and understood instantly why the other vampires deferred to him.

'I am Count Fibula. So, you are the

hunter?' called the vampire sneeringly. 'I thought you were trapped in there.' He flung out his hand and pointed at the jail. 'But it matters not. I will have the pleasure of destroying you in full view of your friends.'

Anthonia saw his gaze abruptly flick to the side to take in Countess Bray and the others as they ran into the square behind her.

'Ahh,' said Fibula scornfully as the new-comers slowed to a halt, 'you have brought an *army* with you. A very *old* army!'

The vampires round Fibula snorted derisively as Bray, Vane, Vinny, Zircon and the other ancient vampires congregated beside Anthonia.

'Your time has come, Fibula!' shouted Bray. 'Your dastardly reign is at an end!'

'Enough!' screamed Fibula abruptly, pointing a bony finger at her. 'You will perish soon like the others, Bray. But first the vampire hunter. Let him prove his worth.' He glared at Zircon as the old vampire started forward. 'And do not try the *anti-voice*, Zircon. 'This is between the hunter and me!'

Fibula's pointing finger was now aimed at

Anthonia. 'Come,' he cajoled, his voice suddenly low and dreamlike. 'You are not my enemy, you are my servant. Come here and kneel before me. Hear my voice. Obey me. Obey me . . .'

Bray glanced anxiously at Anthonia. Fibula was using *the voice*, the hypnotic, persuasive sound that no human could fight against. Anthonia had boasted that she could resist it but *could she*? Bray felt her heart sink as she saw the girl's eyes slowly close.

'Ahh, yes,' Fibula gloated, his yellow fangs showing as his dark lips stretched in a triumphant smile. 'As I thought. Too easy. Too easy! A boy has come to do a man's work!'

Another screech of contemptuous laughter rang out from his henchmen.

Alarmed, Bray reached out and grasped Anthonia's arm and was surprised when the girl shook it off and stepped forward, her eyes springing open.

'Wrong!' she cried. 'I am not only a true vampire hunter, immune to your pathetic drivel, but I am also a girl!' Anthonia flung off her hat and glared defiantly at the uncomprehending Fibula and his shocked minions. Brandishing the stake-darts in the air like short swords she turned to face the jail and shouted, 'You! In the jail! Now's your chance!' And with that she charged towards Fibula.

'The voice did not affect her!' gasped Spitz in astonishment as he took an instinctive step backwards.

Around him the vampires were in disarray: superstitious and fearful of this wild, charging figure.

Bray started running hot on Anthonia's heels, followed by Zircon and his friends, their old faces grim and set for battle.

Fibula recovered quickly and flung his arms out wide as his vampires wavered.

'Stay!' he roared. 'I will deal with her!'

The command was instantly obeyed. Fired by the certainty of their leader, Fibula's forces rallied and stood their ground, ready now to strike down the onrushing figures.

Chapter Forty-three

'She's gone bonkers!' Joe yelped in amazement as he, Muesli and a crush of vampires stared at Anthonia through the broken panes.

'Come on,' cried Muesli, whirling away from the window. He pushed through the throng, his face grim as he caught the expectant looks in his friends' faces. 'It is time for us to be as brave as the girl. We fight . . . *now*!'

'Yes!' bellowed Corpus gleefully as he and the others followed Muesli towards the door. 'About time too!'

They had only taken a few steps when Muesli stopped, peering downwards in the dark.

'Hold,' he said. 'The floor is slippery here. As the vampires stopped he crouched quickly and touched the flagstones. 'It's oil – flowing under the door!'

'They mean to burn the place down,' cried Darceth.

Still at the window, Joe caught a quick movement to his extreme right. Craning his neck to look he gasped as he saw two vampires drop their torches and a quick burst of flame lick upwards. 'Look out, Muesli!' he yelled, spinning round. 'The oil's on fire!'

Muesli and the others leapt backwards just in time as a sheet of flame swept under the door and slithered like a huge fiery snake across the floor of the jail, following the trail of spilled oil. Sudden fireballs erupted as the flames struck two small lamp-oil jugs in the corner, sending blazing plumes shooting up the wall towards the ceiling. Heads twisted round as another serpent of flame slid out from under the hallway door as the oil there ignited too – its flickering tongues licking hungrily up the legs of the table and chairs and along a curtain that hung across an alcove.

'Quickly!' shouted Corpus over the

crackling of the fire as the vampires turned and twisted, desperately trying to avoid the spreading flames. 'Get the door open!'

Muesli and Darceth, hands wrapped in their own cloaks for protection, lifted the bar from the burning door, while Corpus slid back the bolts and wrenched the door wide.

'An end to Fibula!' shouted Alchema, rallying the vampires around her. 'We fight to the finish!'

'To the finish!' they responded with a roar.

Krazul was first out. With a blood-curdling cry he leapt across the river of fire into the misty square and fell on the nearest of Fibula's men. Right behind him were Muesli, Alchema, Sable and Darceth, howling like wolves as they too threw themselves at the enemy. They were quickly joined by the freed prisoners who leapt from the jail to their aid.

Inside the jail Corpus swiftly dragged the trussed jailors to the door and tossed them into the square before turning to kneel beside Joe.

'Come on, Joe!' he cried. 'Up with you. It'll keep you above the fire.'

With Joe clinging to his neck, Corpus instantly leapt across the flames and through the door.

Once outside Joe slid to the ground and Corpus pointed to the alleyway at the side of the jail.

'Round there, Joe,' he cried above the howling and screeching of the fighting vampires. 'There's an outside staircase. You'll be safe at the top!'

Joe hesitated for a fraction of a second, glancing anxiously at the screaming melee only a few metres away. He desperately wanted to help his friends but knew that he wasn't big enough or strong enough to fight a vampire. Turning quickly he ran reluctantly for the alley.

As Joe sprinted away, Corpus turned back to the fray, a look of wild excitement in his eyes.

Chapter Forty-four

Anthonia bore down on Fibula with a defiant cry, thrusting her stake-darts straight at the vampire's heart.

At the last moment Fibula twisted away with a speed that surprised her. As she swept past, carried by her own momentum, Fibula's talons raked her shoulder, sending her tumbling heavily to the ground where she lay, stunned. Fibula spun round, ready to pounce, but a leaping figure suddenly landed between him and his prey.

'You!' he spat out.

'You will not beat me this time, Fibula,' hissed Alchema, her voice rising to a scream as she flew at him. The speed and ferocity of her attack startled Fibula and he had to leap backwards to avoid his face being torn by her slashing talons. Regaining his balance in an instant, he threw off Alchema's clutching grasp and the two vampires circled each other, drifting off the ground at last like great black birds, locked into each other's hate-filled stare.

All around them the battle raged – Fibula's vampires now full of confidence, having taken heart from the fall of the vampire hunter.

From the top of the stone steps at the side of the jailhouse Joe watched the furious struggles – vampire pitted against vampire. His heart lifted when he saw that the two sides seemed to be evenly matched – the intervention of the older vampires having swelled the ranks of the rebels. But gradually his spirits sank again as, one by one, the weakened prisoners and the old vampires were swiftly overcome and struck down. Soon many of them lay groaning on the ground, their faces and clothing spattered with blood, and Joe saw that the odds had easily swung back in Fibula's favour.

All over the square now he could see

instances where two of Fibula's minions were fighting only one rebel.

Anxiously Joe searched the seething mass for Muesli and Corpus. Suddenly he saw them. His two friends were fighting side by side in the centre of the square – Muesli struggling with Horba while Corpus fought a violent battle with Spitz.

The two big vampires were tearing at each other like tigers, leaping, striking home with talons and fists then backing off, circling each other, hissing their hatred, then flying together again.

Muesli fought desperately with Horba. Each had a tight hold on the other. They spun and swayed, twisting and writhing like snakes as each tried to force the other down.

Suddenly out of the struggling crowd below sprang two vampires – one chasing the other. The first vampire leapt on to the wall of the jail right beside Joe and he lurched back in alarm. Joe found himself staring briefly into a pair of dark-purple eyes filled with panic before the vampire leapt away again, his cloak flying, his thin fingers clawing at the stonework. The chasing vampire sprang after him in pursuit, both scurrying up and across the wall as quickly and lightly as two squirrels before disappearing over the edge of the jailhouse roof. With a start Joe realized that the chasing vampire had been none other than Sable . . . the sister of Darceth and Krazul. What a sister to have! he thought.

The mist thinned slightly and swirled upwards for a few seconds, allowing Joe a brief view over the heads of the fighting vampires to the far side of the square. There he glimpsed Vane and, despite the situation, he smiled. He saw that, for the first time in his life, the little werewolf did not have his umbrella over his head outdoors. Instead Vane was rushing about on the fringes of the battle brandishing his trusty brolly like a weapon. Sometimes he used it to hook a leg from under one of Fibula's men and at others to whop an enemy over the head as he struggled with a rebel. Joe's heart leapt. If Vane was there then his dad might be there too.

Yes! There he was, running about on the edge of the battle, anxiously scanning the seething crowd.

He's looking for me, Joe realized.

'Dad!' he called frantically but his shout

was lost in the screeching tumult.

Before Joe could summon the courage to leave his refuge, the mist descended again and Vane and Vinny were lost to view.

The flames from the jail were not so fierce now. Having consumed most of the door and wooden furniture, the fire was now burning itself out against the thick stone walls.

Just then Joe saw Anthonia.

Dazed and bleeding from a shoulder wound, she was trying to crawl through the swarming throng to safety but was being buffeted on all sides. A flying foot caught her in the ribs and she sprawled full length.

Joe gasped in horror as he saw one of Fibula's vampires pounce, clutching at her arm. Without stopping to think, Joe was down the steps in an instant and racing towards Anthonia. Diving and ducking through the battle he threw himself at her assailant in a flying, waist-high rugby tackle. Down they both went, the vampire gasping in surprise as he struck the ground heavily. Joe sprang to his feet but the vampire made a lunge for him.

'It's all right, Joe. I'll get him!' Darceth was suddenly there between Joe and the vampire, fending off the would-be attacker and hurling him again to the ground.

Quickly Joe took Anthonia by the arm and helped her stumble away from the fight. He guided her into the lane towards the staircase he had vacated minutes earlier.

Anthonia sank on to the bottom step, clutching her wounded shoulder. There was also a graze on her forehead where she had struck the ground after Fibula's blow.

'Thank you,' she whispered weakly. She took a deep breath then winced, clutching her ribs. Shaking her head she frowned. 'Oh, I've been so stupid, Joe,' she muttered dispiritedly. 'Had no idea what I was doing. Meddling, that's all it was . . . just meddling. Sticking my nose in where it wasn't wanted.'

'But you were really brave back there, Anthonia,' replied Joe. 'Your charge at Fibula gave the rebels a good start. I'm sure you've made a difference here.'

Above the shrieking of the vampires, Joe thought he heard a thumping sound. Twisting round in alarm he saw a tall figure hobbling quickly towards them along the dark lane.

He sighed with relief as he recognized who it was.

'Grume!'

The one-legged owner of the Café in the Crypt reached them and peered down at Anthonia, quickly taking in her injuries.

'She'll survive . . .' he rasped, pulling a small, leather-covered bottle from the inside pocket of his cape, 'if she drinks this. Knew there'd be a fight so brought the elixir.' He opened the bottle and helped Anthonia take a few sips.

'Feeling better?' he asked.

Anthonia nodded slowly, a look of surprise in her eyes.

'Yes, thanks,' she replied. 'I actually am. Stronger.'

'That wound needs looking at,' Grume said. 'I'll fetch some water.' He straightened up and glanced at Joe. 'I met your father a while back, young lad. He's searching for you.'

'Thanks, I know,' Joe answered. 'I saw him in the square with Vane. He looks OK.'

'Good,' growled Grume. Before limping away again he gave the small bottle to Joe. 'You might need this,' he said.

Chapter Forty-five

Fibula stood panting with exertion. Sweat and blood glistened on his pale, thin face and his eyes glittered with triumph.

Alchema stared back defiantly, her stern face also streaked with blood as she struggled against the vice-like grip that Scabrus and Crusst had on her arms.

'You needed help to defeat me!' Alchema gasped out. 'But you will not defeat us all!'

'You think not?' Fibula spat out contemptuously. 'Look around you.'

Scabrus and Crusst seized her shoulders and roughly spun her round so she could see the battle going on all about them.

It only took a moment for Alchema to

realize that the rebels were indeed losing. All over the square lay defeated vampires – most of them she knew. With a start she realized that Bray was among them, lying face down, the back of her head stained with blood. Alchema looked among the remaining skirmishes feverishly. *Where were Muesli, Corpus and the others?* Then she saw them. Corpus and Spitz had obviously fought almost to a standstill and were slowly circling each other like great, exhausted black bears. Muesli, Sable and a few others had broken away from the battle and had formed a circle to protect the remaining old vampires. They were fending off quick attacks from a screaming crowd – Horba among them – but they looked exhausted and near to defeat.

Out of the corner of her eye she saw Vinny dart into the lane by the side of the jail. She had seen Joe go in there earlier so she felt a faint glimmer of hope that they at least might escape.

'Your rebellion has been crushed, Alchema,' snarled Fibula as she was hauled round to face him again. He flung out a hand to point at Muesli and the small group of survivors still defying his men. 'Once that pathetic, bloodless creature and those remaining traitors have been vanquished there will be no one standing in my way. No one to oppose my plans for the creation of a new vampire empire. The world will once again learn to fear the onset of night.'

Alchema lifted her head proudly.

'Your end will come, Fibula,' she promised. 'Sooner or later.'

'I think not,' sneered Fibula, his dark eyes blazing. 'You see, Countess Alchema . . . *I intend to live forever.*'

Chapter Forty-six

Count Zircon lay wounded and spent among his injured friends as Muesli, Sable and the others tried to fight off the increasingly ferocious attacks of Fibula's minions.

Kneeling beside him were Count and Countess Interra, both near collapse.

Zircon tried to struggle up but Countess Interra laid a hand on his shoulder, gently restraining him.

'Rest,' she murmured, her eyes filled with concern. 'Do not tax yourself.'

The aged count shook his head.

'My time is not long,' he gasped. 'I cannot rest now. Help me to sit up.'

His old friends gripped him by the arms,

carefully pulling him to a sitting position.

Count Zircon peered at the violent struggle going on around them, his breath rasping and shallow.

'We are being defeated, aren't we?' he whispered hoarsely at last.

'It is true,' replied Count Interra slowly and sadly. 'I'm afraid we have failed.'

The oldest vampire in Eyetooth weakly beckoned his friends nearer. When they were close he murmured, 'We may yet have one chance of victory . . .'

'Victory?' breathed the countess, holding Zircon's faltering gaze.

'The *over-voice* . . .' answered Zircon.

Count Interra frowned and his wife shook her head uncertainly.

'The over-voice has not been used for centuries,' she hissed. 'It is too dangerous. It requires enormous mental strength from a number of vampires. The power created can defeat our enemy, yes, but it can also kill those who use it.'

'It is the only hope,' Zircon whispered.

'But,' protested Count Interra looking at the exhausted and aged vampires around them, 'we and our friends here are the only ones who are capable of employing it. But do they have enough strength left? Do we dare?'

'Ask them,' was Zircon's faint reply. 'If they agree then I will lead them.'

'But you can't!' exclaimed the countess. 'It would surely finish you.'

Count Zircon smiled wearily.

'I have enough will remaining to do it,' he responded, his waning voice barely audible. 'It will be my last and best act.'

Chapter Forty-seven

Fibula stared disdainfully at Alchema, his lips twisted in a sneer.

'I will keep you alive until the end, Alchema,' he hissed, 'as a special treat. You will see me send your traitor friends to oblivion one by one.' On either side of Alchema, Scabrus and Crusst sniggered, tightening their grip on her arms. Then suddenly Scabrus's expression changed. His triumphant grin vanished and was replaced by a look of bafflement. He staggered, taking one hand off Alchema's arm and clutching at his throat.

An instant later Crusst released his grip on Alchema completely and bent over, coughing and gasping.

Amazed, Alchema swiftly shook off Scabrus's now limp grasp. She had no idea why she was suddenly free but it didn't matter . . . all she wanted to do was seize Fibula. She tensed, ready to pounce on her enemy but stopped, arms out and fingers spread like claws. *Fibula was choking too!*

And then she heard it – a deep, reverberating, sonorous sound that seemed to well up from the ground like a suffocating fog. Startled, she gazed around her and saw that the mist was being driven by some unseen force into a great, madly speeding cyclone. It was like being in the centre of a whirlpool or the eye of a tornado. Round and round the mist went, faster and faster until it was a spinning wall of cloud.

All fighting stopped. The rebels stood looking around them in dazed amazement as their foes pitched forward on to the ground or staggered about clutching their heads.

Alchema felt light-headed but otherwise unaffected by the penetrating, all-enveloping noise. She saw that the whirling mist was lit from within – a milky phosphorescence that emanated from the group of old vampires protected by Muesli and his friends.

Fibula and his six 'chosen' vampires were worst affected. Spitz and Horba had dropped to their knees, shaking, while Scabrus, Crusst, Sleed and Blech writhed on the ground, their faces contorted in pain.

Fibula himself crouched, shoulders hunched, talons scraping at the rain-slick flagstones as he tried to stop the vibrations that were racking his body. His grey hair hung like wet ropes on either side of his face as his head drooped lower and lower. With a huge effort of will he turned his head and brought his hate-filled eyes to bear on Muesli, only to find his enemy's back was to him.

Chapter Forty-eight

Muesli was gazing in amazement through narrowed and shaded eyes at the glowing brightness that flowed from within the protective cordon. The aged vampires were kneeling together in a tight circle round Zircon, heads touching, eyes shut. From their bodies came a bright luminescence and from their mouths a strange and awe-inspiring sound. It swooped and soared, sometimes a high owl's screech and sometimes a low drone like a hundred lost foghorns drowned in the crashing waves of a winter tempest. He felt a hand touch his arm. He looked up. Sable was beside him. Together they turned and looked across the square.

Fibula and his minions were all on the ground now.

As Muesli, Sable and all their friends watched, awe-struck, great crackles of bright energy rippled through the clouds round them. Twining together, the lines of energy formed seven bolts of twisted lightning that arced down from the whirling, circling mist and struck Fibula and his six 'chosen' ones.

Each of the seven figures was swathed in a searing, white cocoon of light.

From the white intensity that surrounded him, Fibula stared out at Muesli, his eyes two red slits burning with hatred.

Muesli felt the impact of their glare almost like a physical blow.

Slowly, as Muesli and his friends watched in horrified fascination, the seven shapes began to dissolve, each breaking up into a million tiny points of light until finally there was nothing left.

Fibula and his six vampires had utterly vanished.

A moment later, as if with the flicking of a switch, the noise and the light in the mist above them disappeared.

The square was plunged into silent darkness. All was still.

The rebels stood, bewildered, as if coming out of a trance, while around them the remains of Fibula's forces lay stunned.

A low groan behind him cut through the silence and Muesli turned round. In the dim light he saw that the old vampires had collapsed on to the ground and lay gasping for breath. Muesli's friends turned too and quickly went to help. Those who carried little flasks of rats' blood or Fangola passed them round the weakened vampires just as Joe, Vinny and Vane came running up carrying torches.

'Did you see, Muesli? Did you see?' Joe cried. 'Fibula and six of his men . . . *bang* . . . disappeared! Gone!'

'It was incredible,' breathed Vinny. 'Utterly amazing. The light caught them and . . . *zap* . . . that was it.' He gave a low whistle. 'What a shot that would've made – wish I'd had my camera with me.'

The big figure of Corpus emerged from the gloom and joined them. He was bruised and dishevelled but there was a triumphant gleam in his eyes.

'Wouldn't have believed it if I hadn't seen

it with my own eyes, Mooz,' he said quietly, slowly shaking his head at the memory. 'Spitz . . . all of them . . . disappeared into thin air.'

'Muesli!' Sable's voice was tight with concern. 'Count Zircon . . .'

Muesli and Corpus quickly knelt by the prostrate vampire who lay inert, eyes closed, among his drained and exhausted friends. Anxiously they gazed into the pale old face.

Sable touched Muesli's arm gently. 'He's dead, Muesli,' she whispered. 'The effort of leading the over-voice against Fibula and the others was too much for him.'

Muesli and Corpus bowed their heads.

A sobbing cry made everyone turn.

Anthonia stood there, supported on the arm of Grume. She stared in despair at the cold figure of the aged vampire.

'Poor Count Zircon,' she whispered. 'It's all my fault . . .'

'No, my dear,' murmured Countess Interra weakly from where she lay in Sable's cradling arms. 'Zircon chose this path for himself.' She sighed and gazed steadfastly into the distraught girl's eyes. 'And now you can best serve Count Zircon's memory by keeping his secret and ours for as long as you live.'

'You'll do that, won't you, Anthonia,' boomed an unmistakable, if shaky, voice.

'Bray!' cried Muesli in delight as the familiar crumpled figure limped slowly towards them out of the shadows. 'You're all right! I saw you fall . . .'

Bray smiled tiredly as Alchema helped her walk the last few paces.

'A dastardly blow from behind,' she said. 'Raised a lump on my old cranium. But Joe gave me a drink of Grume's excellent elixir and I am revived.' She patted Anthonia's good arm. 'Well, girl?' she asked kindly.

Anthonia hung her head then looked up into the broad, pale face. 'Thank you, Countess,' she replied quietly. 'I don't deserve your kindness.' She turned and gazed at the faces that, not long ago, she would have despised. A saying of her mother's came to her: *Always try to see the whole picture* . . . She had forgotten that advice in her mad, headlong obsession with her great-grandmother's legacy. But now that she had seen the whole picture she understood why Beatrice had turned her back on her quest and returned to a normal life.

Zircon had shown her that some vampires did have feelings just like humans and, more importantly, that *it was very dangerous indeed to meddle in vampires' affairs*. She had been lucky. She had meddled in their affairs and had survived – more than that, she had helped them defeat a great evil. But she would not meddle in their lives again. She took a long, shaky breath. For the first time in a year she felt free.

'I promise to keep your secret for as long as I live,' she said. 'I will not let any of you down.'

Chapter Forty-nine

The battle for Eyetooth was over. Fibula's defeated and dejected followers had been allowed to return to their homes. Without their forceful leader and his six strong henchmen they had lost all will to fight and had easily been persuaded never to disturb the peace of Eyetooth again.

Fibula's servant, Ichor, was a changed person. Granted a pardon, he wandered around blissfully, a broad grin on his face, telling everyone he was going to find a nice little house to live in, where he could warm himself at a roaring fire whenever he liked. He would never be cold again!

The wounded were all taken care of and

helped home – revived by draughts of Grume's elixir and rats' blood.

More than one vampire, however, spurned rats' blood – preferring to drink the herbal Fangola.

Corpus smiled at Muesli.

'Looks like this non-blood-drinking, vegetarian thing is catching on, Mooz. But, so far, not with me.' He sighed in satisfaction as he drained a cup of rats' blood and then raised a glass of Fangola to his lips. 'I like the taste of both.'

Muesli grinned at his old friend.

'Each to his own, Corpy,' he said.

Chapter Fifty

In the ancient burial crypt deep below Eyetooth, the old vampires gathered round the marble tomb of Count Zircon. In each right hand a brightly burning torch was held aloft, the leaping orange flames casting inky-blue shadows among the thick stone pillars and over the arching ribs of the vaulted ceiling. The vampires stood draped in their black cloaks, immobile as statues, heads high, their voices joined in a murmuring chant as they carried out the archaic burial ceremony.

Vinny, Joe and Anthonia were allowed to be present. They stood at the back of the underground chamber, watching in awe as, finally, Muesli and his friends were called forward to pay their last respects.

Joe was transfixed. The quiet dignity and dark mystery of the funeral made the hairs prickle on the back of his neck. He was deeply affected by the sacrifice Count Zircon had made to save the world from Fibula.

Later, as he, Muesli and the others recrossed the jailhouse square after the ceremony, they stopped to gaze around at the scene of the battle.

The door to the jail swung charred and half destroyed on its black hinges, the sooty marks of the fire plain to see on the wall round the doorway and window. On the cold, wet flagstones, however, there was no trace, no mark, to indicate where Fibula and his six chosen vampires had once been.

'They're gone forever, aren't they, Countess Alchema?' asked Joe.

Alchema sighed. 'For a long time at least, Joe,' she replied. 'The over-voice does not destroy – it imprisons.'

'Imprisons?' asked Anthonia. 'Where?'

'Their physical entities have been dispersed and they are now trapped in the nether world of the undead – halfway between life and oblivion,' answered Alchema.

'We had all heard of the over-voice, of course, Alchema,' said Muesli quietly. 'But had never experienced it.'

'It was awesome!' breathed Joe.

'Here's my understanding of it,' boomed Bray, scratching her tangled mane of green curls. 'Fibula and his dastardly minions will remain in the nether world as long as the old vampires' will remains strong. That it, Alchema?'

Alchema smiled at her long-time friend.

'That's precisely it, Bray,' she responded.

'So there's a chance Fibula could come back?' Joe gasped.

Alchema shook her head.

'I hope not, Joe,' she said. 'Once we have elected a new leader of the council . . .' she looked meaningfully at Muesli, 'who might well be you, Muesli, we will try and find a way to make Fibula's imprisonment permanent.'

'I'll be proud to help in any way I can, Alchema,' replied Muesli, 'but as leader . . .? I don't know if I could.'

'Don't be so modest, Mooz!' exclaimed Corpus, slapping his old friend on the back heartily. 'You'd do a great job. I'd vote for you!'

'Me too,' cried Darceth enthusiastically.

'And me,' said his brother.

'If I had a vote it would go to you, Count Muesli,' added Vane. 'But werewolves and servants don't get council votes in Eyetooth.'

'Yes, Vane,' replied Muesli thoughtfully, 'that's something I would change.'

Vane laughed delightedly and, in sudden high spirits, tossed his umbrella high in the air.

'A vote at last!' he cried. 'I never thought it was possible!'

Corpus dodged the falling brolly, caught it and handed it back to the little werewolf.

'Lots of things might be possible if Mooz takes over, Vane,' he said, grinning. 'But getting away with braining a vampire is not one of them.'

Sable touched Muesli's arm.

'Think about it,' she advised quietly. 'You have more support than you think.'

'Of course you have. And I'd like the film rights for the ceremony. What a movie it would make!' cried Vinny, smiling impishly.

The vampires turned to him, startled.

'Only kidding,' he said.

'I think you should do it, Muesli,' said Joe, gazing proudly at his young vampire friend. 'You'd make a cool leader.'

Chapter Fifty-one

Three days later Vinny and Joe did attend a ceremony – but it wasn't Muesli's election as leader. It was the prize-giving ceremony at the film festival ... where Vinny's *Vampires on Holiday* had won the prize for Best Short Film Comedy.

Vinny immediately phoned the rest of the family to tell them the good news.

They were thrilled – especially Joe's Granny Roz.

'This makes up for missing out on the fun up at Eyetooth,' she told Vinny glee-fully. 'I'm going to be a star! Next stop Hollywood!'

They had taken Anthonia to the

ceremony and she was as delighted as every-one else. '*Two* vampire success stories in one week,' she said with a grin. 'Excellent!'

'What are you going to do now, Anthonia?' Joe asked. 'Will you carry on working at the hotel?'

Anthonia shook her head.

'I've decided to go home, Joe,' she replied. 'I haven't seen my mum for nearly a year. It's time we got to know each other again.' Then she smiled mischievously. 'You know what? I think I'll become a hunter again.' Joe and Vinny gave her startled looks but she laughed and said, 'A *fossil*-hunter! I've always been interested in palaeon-tology.' She took a small stone from her jeans' pocket and held it out on her open palm.

Joe looked at the ribbed shape outlined on the stone's flat surface and grinned.

'It's a fossil,' he said.

'A trilobite,' replied Anthonia. 'Picked it up in the tunnels. It means that millions and millions of years ago, the rocks of Eyetooth were under the sea.' She closed her fist round the small stone and smiled at Joe. 'But I'll never tell anyone where I found it. It's another of Eyetooth's secrets that

I'll keep forever.' She held out her hand. 'To our secrets,' she said.

Joe took Anthonia's hand and shook it solemnly. 'To our secrets,' he replied.

Epilogue

With Fibula's defeat, humans are no longer in danger of a vampire attack. How long, though, can the malevolent count be kept imprisoned in the netherworld of the undead? The will of the old vampires needs to remain resolute for this – but will it? Will Muesli and his friends find a way to keep Eyetooth and the human world safe?

In the car on the way home Joe easily pushes all thoughts of Fibula's fate to the back of his mind. Having considered what will happen on the mountain now he is convinced that all will be well. He has great faith in the strength and determination of his vampire friends. Sitting back clutching his dad's award he smiles to himself as he remembers his last hour in Eyetooth.

After the burial ceremony they took a brief rest in Fibula's castle – which Countess Bray had rightfully reclaimed as her own. Joe was delighted to see the countess immediately begin clearing the great hall of its layers of grime and cobwebs – a silk scarf tied over her unruly green curls and a duster in her hand.

While Vinny drank a glass of Fangola with Corpus and Muesli in the Café in the Crypt, Joe and Anthonia explored the castle, starting with the tower room where Joe's family had been imprisoned. From the cell's window they looked out over Eyetooth, marvelling at the darkly huddled rooftops, turrets and spires piercing the mist around them.

Back in the great hall once more, Joe found that Vinny had returned and helped Bray build a roaring fire in the enormous grate. Dozens of candles were burning on wrought-iron candelabra, clean for the first time in years. Fibula's castle had begun its transformation.

Too soon it was time to say their farewells and Muesli and Corpus escorted Joe, his dad and Anthonia down through the tunnels and into the human world again.

'Will you become leader if they want you to, Muesli?' Joe asked as they all stood by the car in the pearly light of dawn.

'I believe I will,' Muesli replied, smiling broadly.

'And I'm looking forward to getting my old job back as Eyetooth's only policeman,' Corpus exclaimed. 'I'm hoping it'll be a fairly quiet line of work from now on.'

'So perhaps,' Joe said awkwardly, 'maybe sometime in the future . . . I might be able to visit Eyetooth again?'

'I think that could be arranged,' Muesli replied kindly, glancing at Corpus who smiled agreement. 'Shall we say in exactly a year's time?'

Joe grins as he twists round in his seat and watches the dark pines and misty mountains recede behind him.

A year. Only a year!

He can hardly wait.

Nerve-tingling, fast-paced adventure with bite!

Count Muesli is the hottest veggie vampire in town. Banished by the evil Count Fibula, Count Muesli must leave Eyetooth. But when his human friends are captured by Fibula, he braves all the dangers and returns to Eyetooth to save them.

'A compelling ride, full of invention, strong characters and constant action'
– Guardian

Dracula is so last century!